JETSONS®

The
Movie

Story Adaptations by Etta Wilson

Illustrations by Bob Singer

Art Direction by Linda Karl

It was a gray misty morning and George Jetson was catching a few extra winks — until Rosie the robot maid rolled in. With a few clicks of her control rod, the lights came on, the drapes opened, and George's bed popped him out on the floor.

"Up and at 'em, Mr. J," she said.

George stepped on the people-mover track. In two minutes he had been showered, dried, toothbrushed, combed, and dressed. Rosie gave him a cube of toast for breakfast, and he was ready to leave for work.

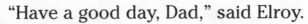

"Have a good day, Dad," said Elroy.
"Love you, Dad," said Judy.
"Bye, dear," said Jane.
"I ruv you, Rorge," said Astro.
"I know, I know. I love you too!" George wiped his face and headed down the exit tube.

After a quick flight in his jetcar, George slid to his desk at Spacely Sprockets. One push of the button and his work was done. Then it was time to report in.

"This is George Jetson," he said to the speaker phone. "What's our old penny-pinching, pea-headed president up to today?"

"Mr. Spacely is meeting with the Board of Directors for the entire day," replied the voice on the phone.

That was George's signal. He leaned back to sleep — for the entire day.

In the board room, Mr. Spacely was telling the Board about his top secret project — the Orbiting Ore Asteroid Manufacturing Plant Unlimited International, Inc. — O. O. A. M. P. U. I. I. for short!

"This new plant on the asteroid produces sprockets at one-tenth of what it costs here," he said. "Soon we will produce our one-millionth sprocket in space!"

The Board cheered Spacely's news.

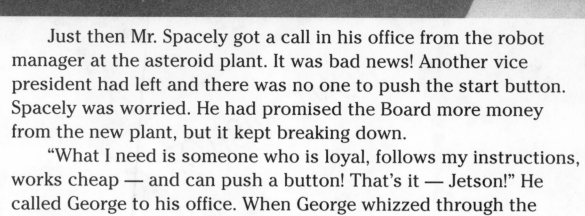

Just then Mr. Spacely got a call in his office from the robot manager at the asteroid plant. It was bad news! Another vice president had left and there was no one to push the start button. Spacely was worried. He had promised the Board more money from the new plant, but it kept breaking down.

"What I need is someone who is loyal, follows my instructions, works cheap — and can push a button! That's it — Jetson!" He called George to his office. When George whizzed through the door, Spacely greeted him with a big smile.

"Welcome aboard, Vice President Jetson!"

"Me? Vice President?" George was dazed.

"I knew you were the right man for the job up there! With your family beside you, you face a new challenge — a new button to push — in space!"

JETSON

9

At Elroy's school, the basketball game was all tied up. The coach looked down the bench and called Elroy to go in.

"Shall I give 'em the Elroy Elevator shot, Coach?"

"What else? It's the only shot you got! Get out there and sink it!"

Elroy dribbled and faked. "Going up, Going down! Going up! Going down! Going in!"

But the ball didn't go in and the game ended! Elroy's team lost!

"My life is over!" Elroy cried as he left the gym alone.

Meanwhile, Judy had joined her friends at the teen hangout to dance to the music of their favorite rock singer — Cosmic Cosmo. Suddenly Cos came over to dance with Judy.

"Hey, what's your name?" he asked.

"Ju-Ju-Judy," she stammered.

"Well, Ju-Ju-Judy, we've got a date Friday night!"

Judy squealed with delight. "Imagine! A date with Cosmic Cosmo!"

George had big news for the family when he got home that
night. "They made me a vice president! We're moving to Spacely's
Orbiting Ore Asteroid — tomorrow!"

"Move? But, George, I'm redecorating here," said Jane.

"But, Daddy, I've got a date with Cosmic Cosmo!" cried Judy.

"I'll start packing!" said Elroy.

"Hey, I thought you'd be happy," said George. "I'm a vice
president!"

"Maybe it won't be so bad, dear," Jane said.

Early the next day, the Jetsons were zooming off to their new home on the asteroid.

"There it is!" yelled Elroy.

"Look, Judy, it's got a shopping mall!" Jane said.

"And there's the new plant!" said George.

"*Your* new plant, Mr. Vice President!" Jane replied.

When the Jetsons walked into their new apartment, they found — nothing! It was empty and bare.

"Where's my room?" asked Elroy.

"Where's the phone!" asked Judy.

"I wonder if this works up here," Rosie said as she held up her control rod and clicked it a few times.

Things started to happen fast. Lights came on, beds shot out of the wall, a complete kitchen rolled in — even a telephone flipped down for Judy!

"Oh, wow! This is nebular!"

Just then the doorbell rang. It was Lucy 2, their new neighbor. "You'll meet my husband, Rudy 2, at the plant. And we have a son, Teddy 2. We were built as a complete family unit," she said. "I want to show you around the mall tomorrow."

Life on the asteroid was looking better all the time!

Later that day Elroy brought home a strange new pet. George and Jane were trying to decide who he might belong to when two large creatures just like the little one appeared at the door.

"We're the Furbelows, Bertie, Gertie, and that's our little Fergee. She's a girl. We live next door."

"We're pleased to meet you," Jane replied.

16

It was quiet that night at the orbiting ore plant until, all at once, there were little sounds like the scratching of mice feet, and tiny beams of light in the dark shadows . . .

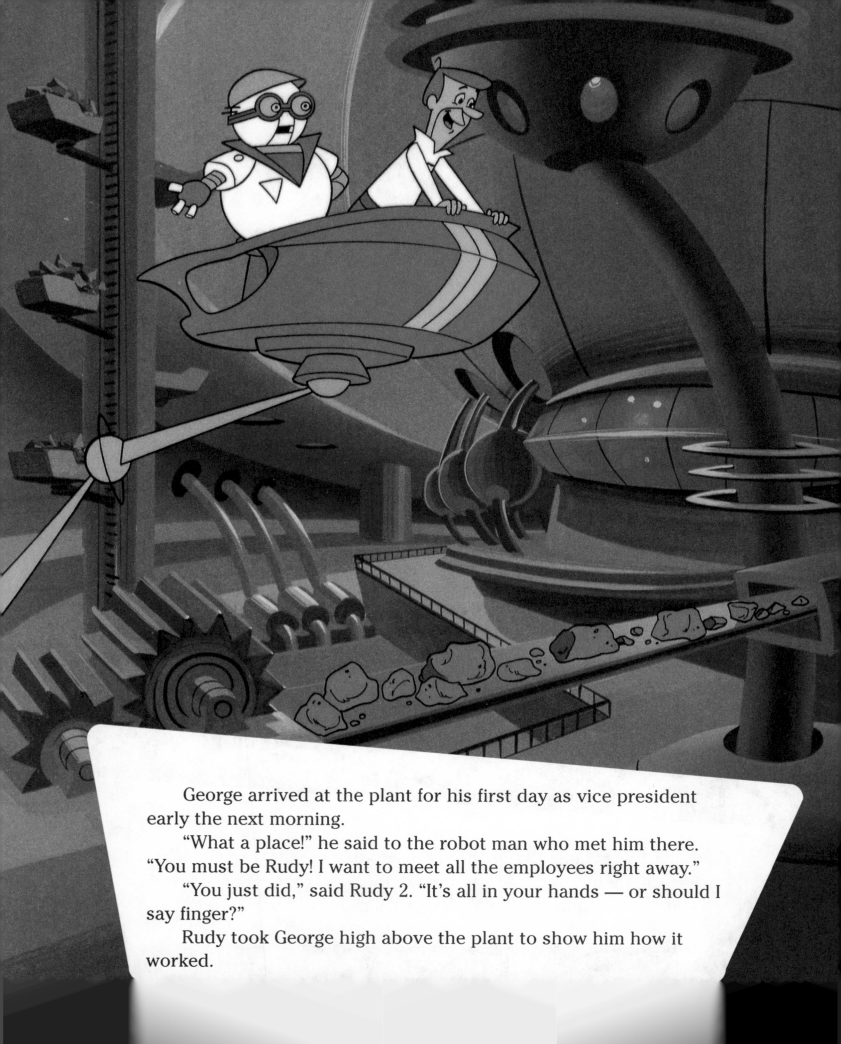

George arrived at the plant for his first day as vice president early the next morning.

"What a place!" he said to the robot man who met him there. "You must be Rudy! I want to meet all the employees right away."

"You just did," said Rudy 2. "It's all in your hands — or should I say finger?"

Rudy took George high above the plant to show him how it worked.

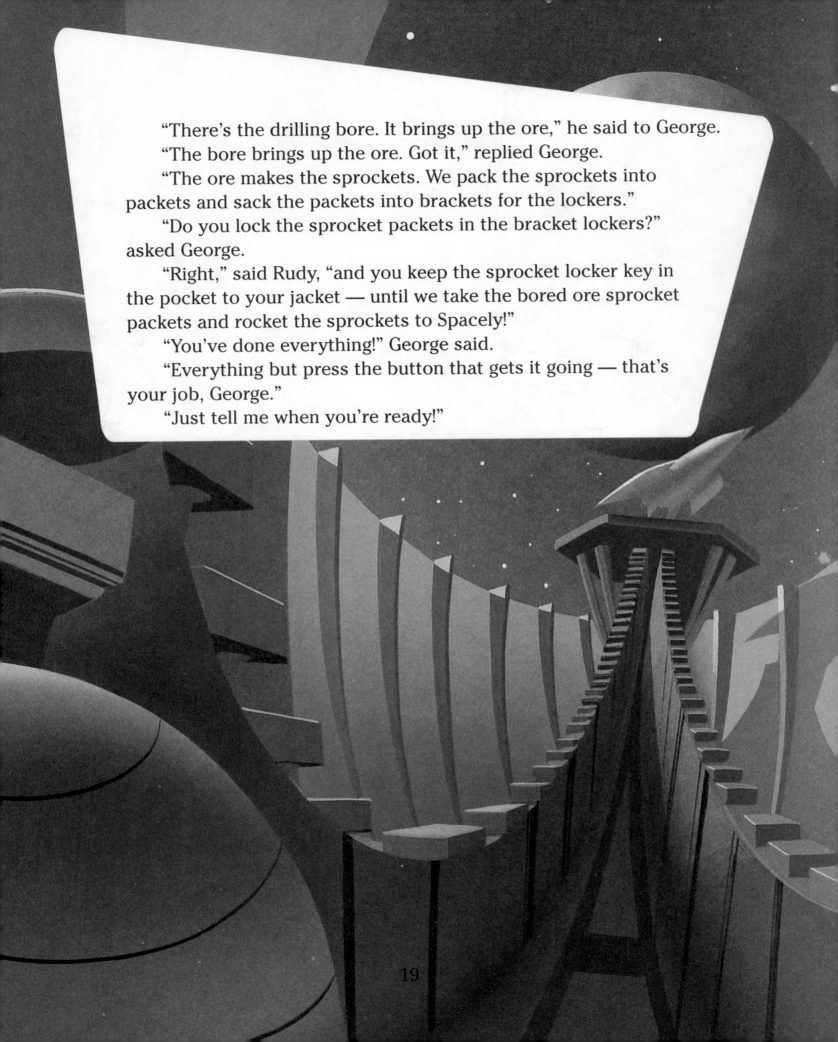

"There's the drilling bore. It brings up the ore," he said to George.

"The bore brings up the ore. Got it," replied George.

"The ore makes the sprockets. We pack the sprockets into packets and sack the packets into brackets for the lockers."

"Do you lock the sprocket packets in the bracket lockers?" asked George.

"Right," said Rudy, "and you keep the sprocket locker key in the pocket to your jacket — until we take the bored ore sprocket packets and rocket the sprockets to Spacely!"

"You've done everything!" George said.

"Everything but press the button that gets it going — that's your job, George."

"Just tell me when you're ready!"

19

Meanwhile Lucy 2 was showing Jane and Judy the asteroid mall. "Here we are — the Galaxy Galleria!"

Judy was impressed. "I'd sort of like to wander around by myself," she said.

"Go ahead, dear," said Jane. "Just be back in time for us to get to the plant for Dad's big button-pushing."

Judy was scooting down the spiral elevator on her floating disc, trying to see as much as she could. But she didn't see the boy up ahead until she smashed into him!

"Ow! You dum — duhhh!" She stopped for a closer look.

"Dummy?" he asked with a laugh. "Actually, my name's Apollo Blue."

"I'm Judy. Oh, I've got to go. It's two minutes to twelve."

"See you tomorrow, pumpkin. Same time, same place?" Apollo called.

MOVIES

22

At Elroy's school on the asteroid, the boys played basketball much like they did on earth. The coach paired Elroy against Teddy 2 for some one-on-one.

"My name may be Teddy 2, but I'm number one in this game," he said to Elroy.

"You mean you were number one. Watch my elevator shot!"

Elroy dribbled and faked. "Going up! Going down! Going up! Going down! Going in!"

"No way!" yelled Teddy 2 as his mechanical arm zoomed out to catch the ball.

Elroy was stunned!

"Coming to the ceremony at the plant?" asked Teddy 2.

"You bet!" replied Elroy.

Everyone was at the plant at noon. George stood at the control panel ready to push the button and make the millionth sprocket on the orbiting ore asteroid plant.

Mr. Spacely and the Board were watching from earth.

"Okay, Jetson, push the button!" called Spacely.

The sprocket counter read 999,998 and then 999,999 . . .

"Here it comes! One million sprockets!" yelled George.

Suddenly a sprocket went sailing past George's head. The counter started going backwards. Then sprockets started flying all around. George tried to catch the flying sprockets, but they were coming too fast! Elroy saw one of them hit Teddy 2 and raced over to help him up. Then Rudy 2 hurried the families out of the plant.

"Jetson, you're destroying my plant! Turn that machine off!" yelled Spacely.

"Yes sir! Right away, sir!"

"And get it started soon! Lost time means lost vice presidents!"

Back at the Jetsons' apartment the two families were treating their wounds after the disaster. Rudy 2 tried to explain to George that strange things kept happening at the plant.

"You mean they're not accidents?" asked George.

"No, they were a warning — to close the plant down. That's why Spacely's had four vice presidents. They all had accidents like today — and left!"

"Well, I'm not leaving!" George said. "If someone's sneaking in at night to foul things up, I'm going back tonight and keep watch! George Jetson is taking charge!"

Elroy and Teddy 2 were now best friends. As they heard their dads talking, Elroy had an idea.

The plant was dark that night when George returned.
"All right, you vandals, now you've got George Jetson to deal with!"
George searched the plant high and low with his flashlight and
then sat down at his desk to wait. He was soon sound asleep.

The skittering and scurrying of little feet didn't wake him — even when the little creatures carried him off in the dark.

"My Dad needs help." Elroy said to Teddy 2. "I'm going to the plant and help him solve the mystery of those accidents. All I need is my detecto kit."

"And me," said Teddy 2. "With my elevator shot, we can go through the vent into the plant."

"Wow! Let's go!" Elroy said with a laugh. "Going up! Going up! Going in!"

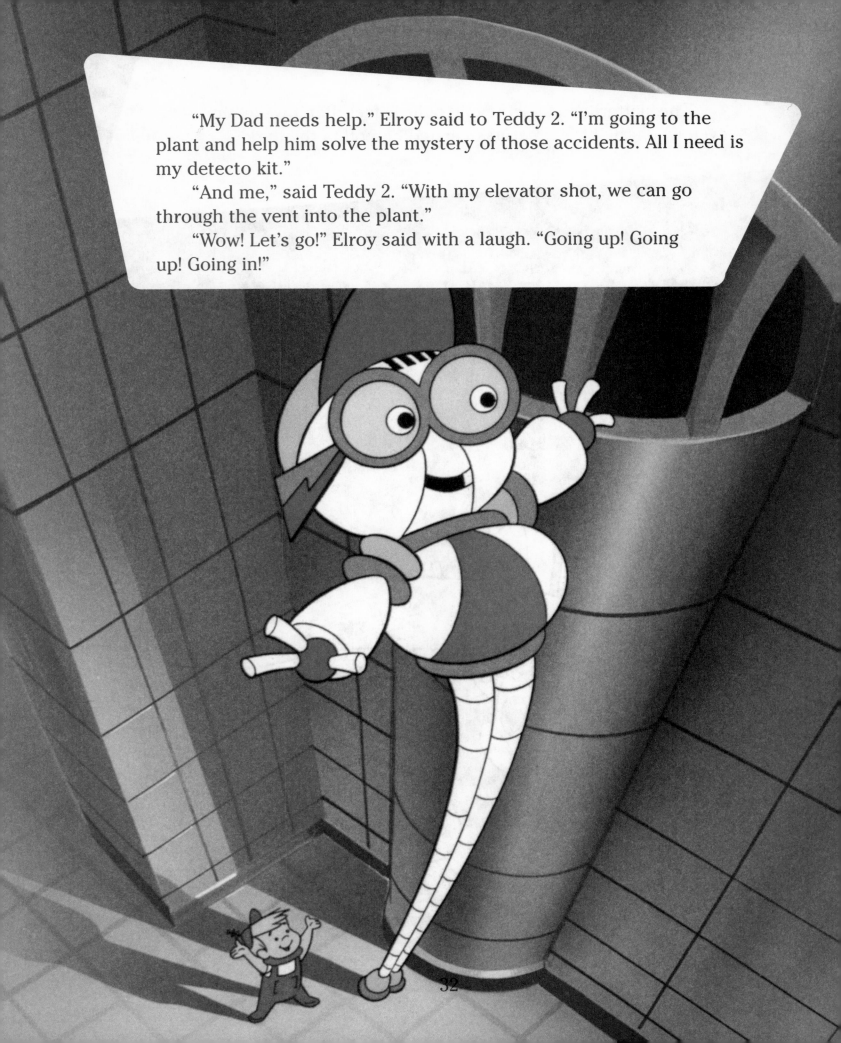

32

As the boys slipped inside, they surprised the little creatures in the dark. Elroy's flashlight passed over them quickly.

"Squeep! Shh!" They scurried off — all except one!

"What was that noise?" asked Elroy.

"Look! Those buckets are moving!"

Each of the boys snatched up a bucket. Under one they found Fergee Furbelow, who pointed to the creature under the other and said, "Grunchee!"

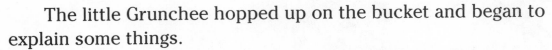

The little Grunchee hopped up on the bucket and began to explain some things.

"Grunchee deedle de dum de . . . WHAM! Whee! Whaaa! Whump!"

"I'm programmed for most languages," said Teddy 2, "and I can tell you that the Grunchee people are not very happy with us. His name is Squeep, and he says we've been destroying their town with the orbiting ore drill."

"My dad wouldn't do that! I want to see for myself!"

Squeep thought for a second, then nodded and pointed toward the buckets on the ore machine that went below the plant floor.

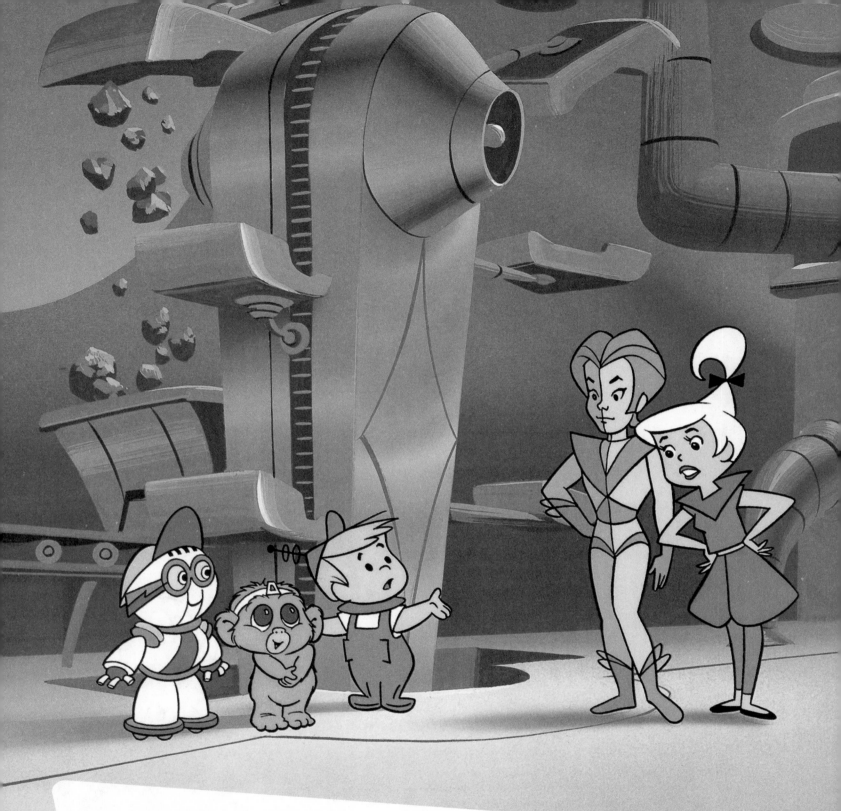

"Elroy Jetson!" Judy called.

She and Apollo had come looking for the boys when Jane discovered they were not at home asleep.

"Well, Well! What have we got here?" asked Apollo.

"He's a Grunchee," said Elroy. "And he's going to show us why the plant keeps having accidents. Come with us, will you, guys?"

"Let's go!" Apollo helped Judy into one of the buckets.

36

Slowly the bucket went down into the dark center of the asteroid.
"Teddy, are you programmed to be scared?" Elroy asked.
"No."
"I am!" said Elroy.

As the bucket stopped on the cavern floor, the kids saw hundreds
of tiny lights go on in the dark shadows. The entire cavern was full
of Grunchees! And they were all looking at the kids in the bucket!

Squeep hopped out quickly and led the rest of them across the cavern through the maze of Grunchee homes.

Judy was looking straight ahead.

"Oh, no!" she exclaimed, "We're destroying their homes!"

The sharp point of the huge drill from the plant above had bored through the ceiling. Piles of rocks and ore had crashed into some of the homes. It was a sad sight.

Up in the plant, Jane, Rudy 2, and Astro had come to look for George and the boys. Astro sniffed for familiar smells near the shaft.

"Relroy! Rorge!" He barked and jumped into one of the ore buckets.

Jane joined him and the bucket went down to the cavern.

"There you are, Elroy Jetson," said Jane. "Now we've found everybody except George."

Suddenly George hopped into the cavern. His hands and feet were tied.

"George, what happened?" Jane peeled the tape off his mouth.

"I was kidnapped by those vicious little furballs!"

"Daddy, they were just trying to save their homes." Judy said.

"Um, George dear," said Jane, "I think we need to have a little talk before I untie you." Then Jane leaned over to whisper in George's ear.

"NO! NO! NO! NO! And that's final!"

"George, all I ask is that you look around and see what your job is making you do. No job is worth that."

Up above in the plant, there was a familiar yell. "Jetson! Jetson!"
Mr. Spacely had taken the first cheap flight to the asteroid.
"Why is this plant shut down?" he asked Rudy 2. "I want my one
millionth sprocket if I have to make it myself. The Board expects
more money!"

Before Rudy 2 could stop him, Spacely pushed the red button
on the control panel and the giant drill bit started to turn.

With each turn the drill dug deeper into the cavern below! The whole place began to rumble and shake. Cracks opened like an earthquake. Rocks fell and a huge chunk of ore broke away from the ceiling. Jane looked at the pile of rubble where Elroy and Squeep had been standing.

"Elroy!" she screamed.

"Squeep! Ibblroy! Wooooop! Ibbble! Grunchee!"

Quick as a wink, a group of Grunchees knew what to do.

They formed a chain and burrowed into the rubble.

43

Elroy came out of the pile headfirst, and in his hand was little Squeep!

"Thanks! Thank you very much!" said George. "Come on, all of you. We've got work to do."

With everyone close behind him, George raced up to the plant control panel.

44

"What are you doing, Jetson?" yelled Spacely. "Stay away from that button!"

"No, sir, Mr. Spacely!" George leaned over and pushed the OFF button. "Did you know about those wonderful little creatures who live below the plant?" George saw the look on Spacely's face.

"Why, you money-grabbing old goat. You did know! Well, let me tell you, these creatures just saved my boy's life. They've got hearts. They care, but you wouldn't know about that, would you?"

"Stop it! Stop it! I can't stand any more!" said Spacely.

"Then figure a way to keep the plant and let the Grunchees have their homes too. It's the only way you'll ever get your millionth sprocket!"

The very next day everyone watched proudly as the Grunchees worked the sprocket machines. The sprockets came out sparkling and perfect. Best of all, the Grunchees' homes were safe.

"I don't believe it. They've doubled production!" said Mr. Spacely.
George watched the sprocket counter carefully.
"999,999 . . . 1,000,000!"
Cheers and shouts rang through the plant.
"Jetson, it's time to plan your trip home. You've done enough here," said Spacely.
"Yes sir, Mr. Spacely, but will I be a vice president?"
"Oh, all right! But no raise!"

The Jetsons were soon headed home to earth in their jetcar. With many hugs, promises to visit, and a few tears, they said goodbye to all their new friends on the asteroid. As the car pulled out into space, Elroy looked back.

"Look, Dad! It's the Grunchees on the roof of our apartment!"

And there they were — waving and flashing their lights and calling, "Thanks, George."

"Well, that sure is nice of them," George said as he blinked a tear from his eye.

HUCKLEBERRY HOUND™
FARMER HUCK

Written by Ronald Kidd
Layouts by Don Ferguson
Paintings by Diana Wakeman

Once upon a time, there was a farm. And on this farm there was a house. And in this house there was a bed. And on this bed there was a farmer.

But it wasn't Old MacDonald.

It was Huckleberry Hound. Huck was fast asleep. And he wasn't calling, "Ei-i-ee-i-oh." Instead, he was snoring.

But not for long.

Suddenly there was a loud clanging noise. Huck looked up sleepily. "Well, sir. Either that's the alarm clock, or my house is on fire," he said.

He sniffed the air, then checked to see if his bed was in flames. "Hmm. Must be the clock."

Yawning, Huck shut off the alarm and climbed out of bed. "Oh, my darlin', oh my darlin', oh my darlin' Clementine..." he sang as he stumbled toward the kitchen.

Across a cornfield, in a tall oak tree, another alarm clock rang.
Two crows, Iggy and Ziggy, awoke with a start.

"Rise and shine!" said Iggy.

"Early bird catches the worm!" said Ziggy.

They flew to the ground and enjoyed a breakfast of fat,
juicy earthworms.

After breakfast, Iggy and Ziggy perched on a fencepost.

"Where is he?" said Iggy.

"I hate it when he's late," said Ziggy.

As they spoke, the farmhouse door opened, and a sleepy Huck
came walking across the cornfield, holding a cup of coffee.

"Mornin', fellas," he drawled.

"Mornin'," the crows replied.

Huck settled back against a tree and took a sip of coffee.
"How's the family?"

"Just fine, thanks," said Iggy.

"I've got pictures of the kids," said Ziggy. The crows
fluttered down and showed Huck a stack of family photos.

"Look how big they're getting," said Huck.

58

R-e-e-e-e-e-t! A loud whistle sounded, and everything changed. Huck leaped to his feet. "Outa my cornfield, you corny crows!" he yelled.

He chased them around the tree and away from the cornfield. But he didn't chase them far enough.

They flew high above the field, then came zooming along the rows of corn, eating as they went.

They munched and they crunched. They chomped and they chewed. They nibbled and they gnawed. Then they perched on the fencepost and laughed and laughed and laughed.

Then they looked around.

"Where did he go?" said Iggy.

"I don't know," said Ziggy.

A moment later, a strange figure came walking up to them.
He had a badge and a funny-looking beak.

"Bird police," he said. "I'm afraid I have to take y'all in."

"For what?" asked Iggy.

"Pluckin' corn in a no-pluckin' zone."

62

Just then his beak slipped off.

"You're not the bird police," said Ziggy. "You're Huck!"

"Consarn crows!" said Huck, as he lunged for them. But Iggy and Ziggy were too quick and got away.

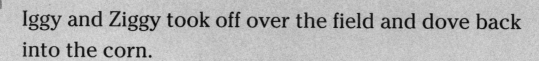

Iggy and Ziggy took off over the field and dove back into the corn.

They munched and they crunched. They chomped and they chewed. They nibbled and they gnawed. Then they perched on the fencepost and laughed and laughed and laughed.

A few minutes later, Iggy noticed something under one of the trees. It was a giant ear of corn! He and Ziggy flew in for a closer look and saw that it was a trap. The corn, made of cardboard, was attached to one end of a rope. At the other end, hanging above the corn, was a box.

"Watch this," said Ziggy. He took out a dollar bill and tucked it under the giant ear of corn. Then the two crows hid behind the tree and waited.

Free

Soon, Huck came along to check his trap. "This oughta fix them crow critters," he said. Then he stopped. "Well, I'll be doggone — a dollar bill. Must be my lucky day."

As Huck leaned over to pick it up, the box fell on top of him. From underneath the box, a muffled voice said, "Then again, maybe not."

Iggy and Ziggy did a little tap dance on top of the box, then hurried back to the cornfield.

They munched and they crunched. They chomped and they chewed. They nibbled and they gnawed. They left a long trail of corncobs as they went along on their *corntravaganza*!

Iggy and Ziggy perched on the fencepost and rested for a while. Then they flew back to the cornfield for dessert. But this time they stopped short. Standing in their way was a tall, strange figure. It was a scarecrow.

"I'm scared!" said Iggy nervously.

"Me, too!" said Ziggy.

They looked at each other and said, "That's why they call it a scarecrow!"

70

But there was *something* very familiar about the scarecrow.
It had a long nose and floppy ears, and it was humming
"Clementine."

71

Iggy and Ziggy grinned at each other.

"This scarecrow needs a little sprucing up," said Iggy.

"Especially around the face," said Ziggy.

Using markers, they turned his frown into a smile. They added a mustache, some freckles, and a pair of glasses.

"Boo, y'all," said the scarecrow. Somehow it wasn't very scary to Iggy and Ziggy.

72

So the two crows munched and they crunched. They chomped and they chewed. They nibbled and they gnawed. Then they perched on the fencepost and laughed and laughed and laughed.

Then Ziggy saw something in the distance. "Let's go investigate," he said to Iggy. When the crows got to the cornfield, they found a sign.

**Warning: Eating corn
may be hazardous to your health.**

"That's funny!" said Iggy.
"Very funny!" said Ziggy.
And they laughed and laughed and laughed.

76

As they howled with laughter, a rope dropped over their heads and tightened around them. They looked up to see Huck on the tree branch.

"Shoulda paid attention to the sign," he drawled. "Adios, you corn crooks, you!"

R-e-e-e-e-e-t! At that moment the whistle blew, and Huck untied the rope. "Well, fellas, we done did a good day's work."

"So long, Huck," said Iggy.

"See you tomorrow," said Ziggy.

"Bright and early, boys," Huck replied.

"Good folk, that Huck," said Iggy.

"The best," said Ziggy.

As the sun set over the cornfield, Huck picked up his coffee cup and headed home.

THE FLINTSTONES™

Story Adaptations by Etta Wilson

Illustrations by Bob Singer

Art Direction by Linda Karl

Fred's Birthday

It was Fred Flintstone's birthday, but he was not very happy as the day began.

"Yeah, some happy birthday this will be! There's no muss or fuss or sign of a party. Maybe Wilma's going to surprise me," he said to himself.

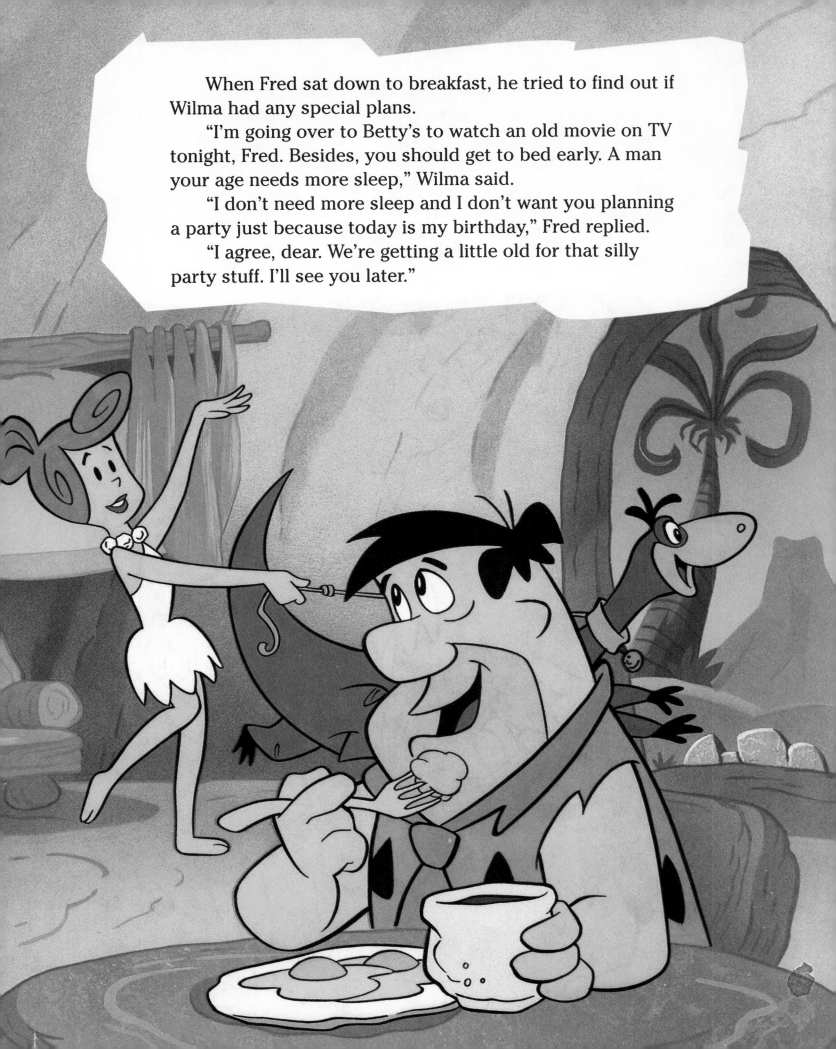

When Fred sat down to breakfast, he tried to find out if Wilma had any special plans.

"I'm going over to Betty's to watch an old movie on TV tonight, Fred. Besides, you should get to bed early. A man your age needs more sleep," Wilma said.

"I don't need more sleep and I don't want you planning a party just because today is my birthday," Fred replied.

"I agree, dear. We're getting a little old for that silly party stuff. I'll see you later."

Wilma ran next door to the Rubbles' where she and Betty and Barney were getting ready for Fred's surprise party that night.

"Have you got it all straight, Barney?" asked Wilma. "You've got to keep Fred from finding out."

"Sure thing, Wilma. First I take him to the golf course; second, to the health club; and third, back here in time for the party."

Back at the Flintstones', Fred had given up looking for his present from Wilma, but he did find a list beside the telephone. It said: "Things to take for Fred's party."

"Ah-hah! So Wilma is gonna surprise me. I bet I can get Barney to tell me about it when we go play golf."

Barney and Fred played all morning, but Barney didn't say a word about Fred's party.

"Come on, Barney. I've had enough golf. Let's go home," said Fred.

"We gotta go to the clubhouse first, Fred."

When Fred heard that, he was certain his party would be in the clubhouse.

"I'll go in first, Barney," he said. "Yahoo, everybody! I'm here!"

But the clubhouse was empty.

"We got here too early, huh, Barney?"

"Too early for what, Fred? I just wanted you to see my new weights."

Fred had guessed wrong!

Next Barney took Fred to the new health center.

"I'll bet that's where they're having my party," Fred said to himself.

"I've got a surprise for you, Fred," Barney said. "Stand up here and close your eyes."

Running on the treadmill was not the surprise Fred expected.

"Shut this thing off, Barney!" he yelled.

Barney let Fred run for a long time before he shut the treadmill off.

"Boy, I'm really beat," Fred said.

"You need a little steam to relax, Fred. Let's have a little snooze."

Back at the Rubbles', Wilma and Betty were starting to worry. Everyone was there for the party — except Barney and Fred.

"I wonder where the boys are. They're an hour late," Betty said.

"I'm so embarrassed, Betty. We can't ask this houseful of people to keep waiting for Fred. We'll have to look for him."

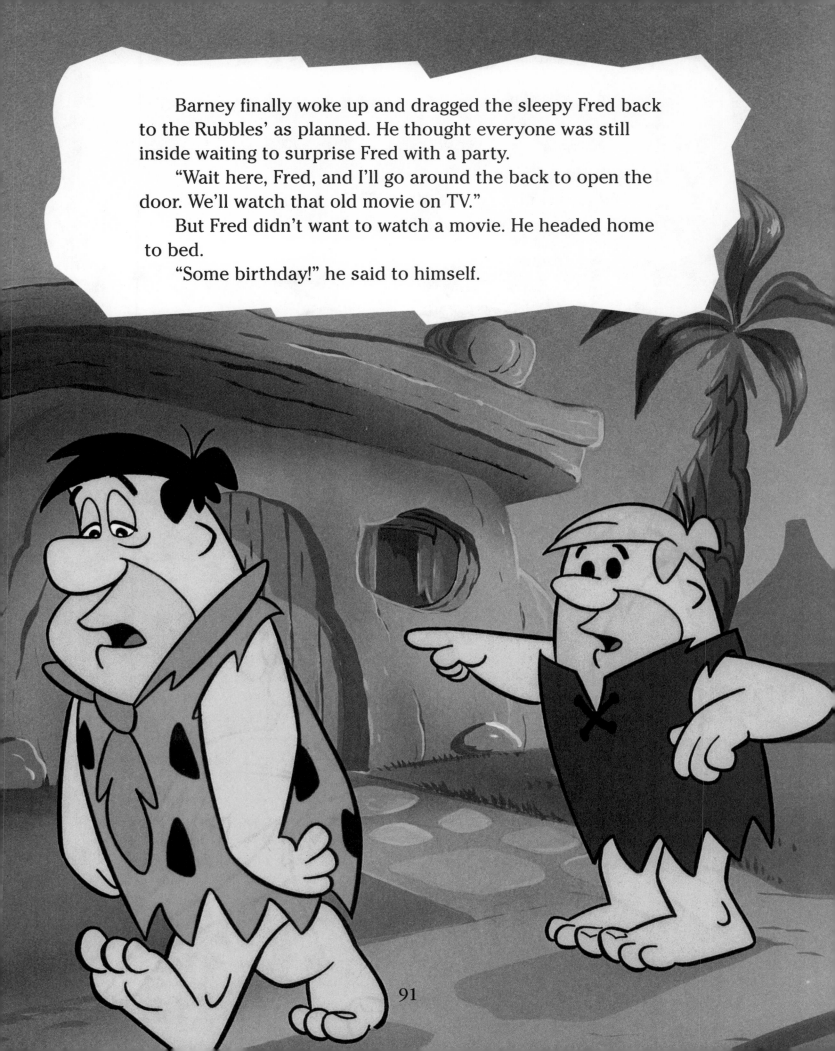

Barney finally woke up and dragged the sleepy Fred back to the Rubbles' as planned. He thought everyone was still inside waiting to surprise Fred with a party.

"Wait here, Fred, and I'll go around the back to open the door. We'll watch that old movie on TV."

But Fred didn't want to watch a movie. He headed home to bed.

"Some birthday!" he said to himself.

When he walked into the living room, he found Wilma crying her heart out.

"Oh, Fred, where have you been? We all planned a party for you but we couldn't find you."

"What's it matter, sweetheart?" Fred replied. "It's still my birthday and we're together. That's all that counts."

Suddenly the door opened.

"Surprise, Fred!"

"Surprise, Flintstone!"

"The surprise party worked after all, Wilma," said Betty.

"Happy birthday, old buddy," Barney said to Fred.

"What do you think of the cake?"

"YABBA-DABBA-DOO!" said Fred.

X-Ray Excitement

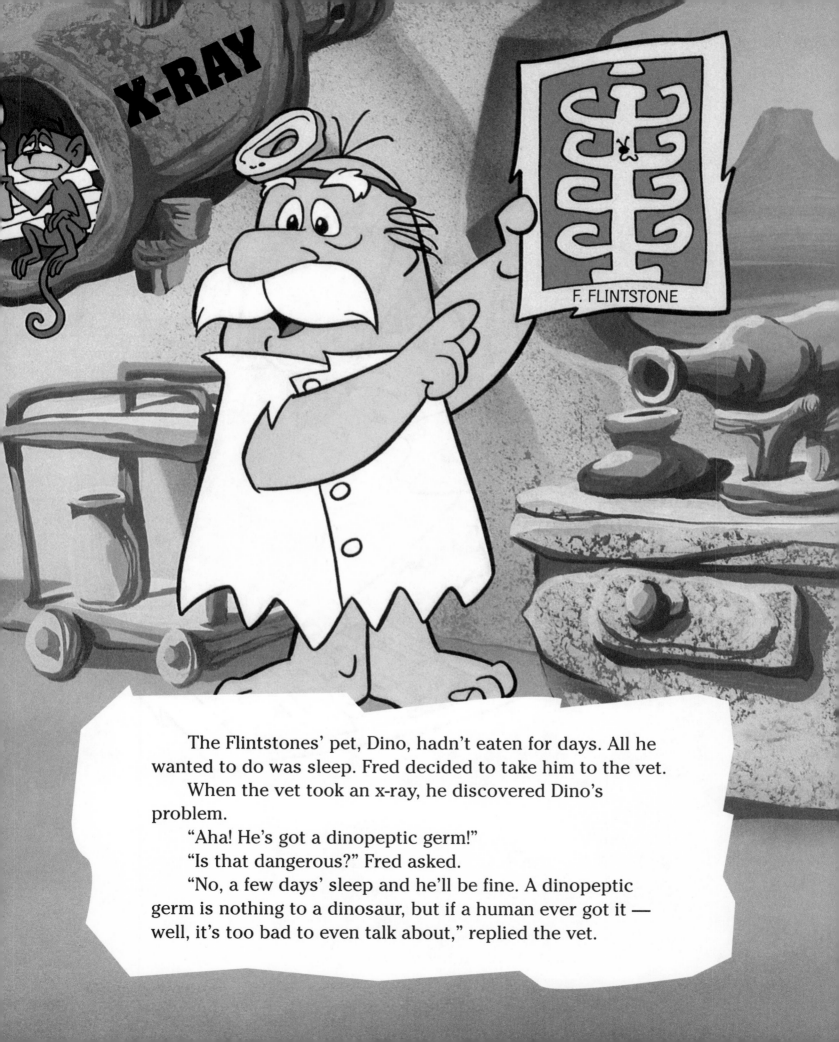

The Flintstones' pet, Dino, hadn't eaten for days. All he wanted to do was sleep. Fred decided to take him to the vet.

When the vet took an x-ray, he discovered Dino's problem.

"Aha! He's got a dinopeptic germ!"

"Is that dangerous?" Fred asked.

"No, a few days' sleep and he'll be fine. A dinopeptic germ is nothing to a dinosaur, but if a human ever got it — well, it's too bad to even talk about," replied the vet.

After Fred and Dino left, the x-ray with Fred's name on it blew out the window. A policeman found it on the street and took it to the doctor at police headquarters.

"Does this x-ray show anything, Doc?" he asked.

"Oh, yes, yes! This man Flintstone has a dinopeptic germ. He must be kept awake for 72 hours so the germ cannot attack him. You'd better go and explain to his wife."

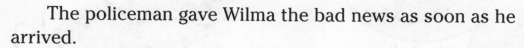

The policeman gave Wilma the bad news as soon as he arrived.

"Mrs. Flintstone, this x-ray shows that your husband has dinopeptitis. But he can be saved. You must see that he doesn't sleep for 72 hours."

"Oh, I will, I will. Thank you," said Wilma.

F. FLINTSTONE

She ran next door to ask Betty and Barney to help her keep Fred awake.

"Remember, we mustn't let him know he's in danger," she told them.

"We'll be over right after dinner and go out someplace," Betty said. "We have to do it for Fred."

"Besides, he owes me twelve bucks!" said Barney.

Fred was tired after a hard day at the quarry. All he wanted was a hot shower before he hit the sack.

"You can't go to bed, Fred," said Wilma. "We have a date to go out with Betty and Barney."

"Yahoo, Freddie Boy," called Barney. "We'll have a ball tonight!"

"Isn't this fun, Fred?" Wilma asked. Fred kept dancing but he was too sleepy to answer.

"Fred, keep your eyes open," said Barney when they sat down to eat. "Here, drink some nice hot coffee."

"I don't want coffee. It keeps me awake. Let's go home!"

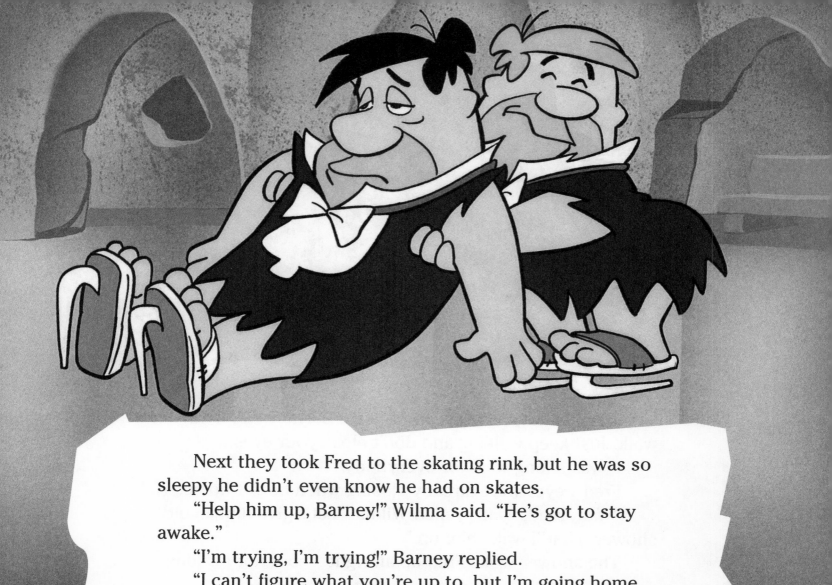

Next they took Fred to the skating rink, but he was so sleepy he didn't even know he had on skates.

"Help him up, Barney!" Wilma said. "He's got to stay awake."

"I'm trying, I'm trying!" Barney replied.

"I can't figure what you're up to, but I'm going home to bed! Anybody want a ride?" Fred asked.

"The car is out of gas, Fred," said Barney. "We'll have to walk. Just keep walking and don't close your eyes."

It was a long walk for everybody.

Fred's eyes were already closing when he got home.

"Wait, Fred, wait!" yelled Wilma. "Let's give him a cold shower. That'll wake him up."

The shower woke Fred up all right — but not for long.

"You'll have to tell him what the trouble is, Wilma," said Barney. "It's the only way to save him."

"You're right. Fred, the doctor showed me your x-ray. He says if you fall asleep, you're a goner!"

"A goner! Oh, no! Do something! Barney, get me some coffee! The doctor said my x-ray —"

"Hold it! Hold it! I never had an x-ray!"
"Yes, you did," said Wilma. "Here it is. It's got your name on it. You had a dinopeptic germ."
"This is Dino's x-ray!" said Fred.

"You mean we kept you awake all night for nothing?" asked Barney.

"Forget it, Barney," said Wilma. "Let's not wake him up again till morning!"

The Blessed Event

THE
FLINTSTONES

Fred and Wilma Flintstone have just come home from the doctor's office.

"Isn't it wonderful, Fred?" said Wilma. "Dr. Rockpile says we can expect the baby any day now."

"Right! Any day now! Are you sure you're okay, Wilma? Let me help you out of the car. You should be resting."

Fred was trying not to worry.

Fred's next-door neighbor, Barney Rubble, was mowing his lawn. Fred ran over to stop the noise.

"Shut that thing off. Wilma needs quiet!"

"Boy, Fred, you sure are one nervous father," said Barney.

"Me? Nervous? Don't be ridiculous!" Fred yelled.

As soon as Fred and Wilma walked into the house, he insisted that she lie down.

"You've got to stay calm and quiet, Wilma. Outside, Dino! I don't want any dog barking."

"Fred, put me down!" Wilma said.

"You need rest and quiet, Wilma. I'll see that you get it!"

But Fred had forgotten to stop the alarm clock.

"Quiet, I said!" he yelled.

When Barney and Betty came over the next day, Fred was pacing the floor.

"You'd better sit down, Fred. You're wearing a groove in the floor," Barney said.

"Look at Wilma out in the yard. She's so calm. All she has to do is tell me she's ready."

"What do you have to do, Fred?" asked Betty.

"I gotta call the doctor, get the car, grab the suitcase, put Wilma in the car, drive to the hospital. She hardly does anything at all."

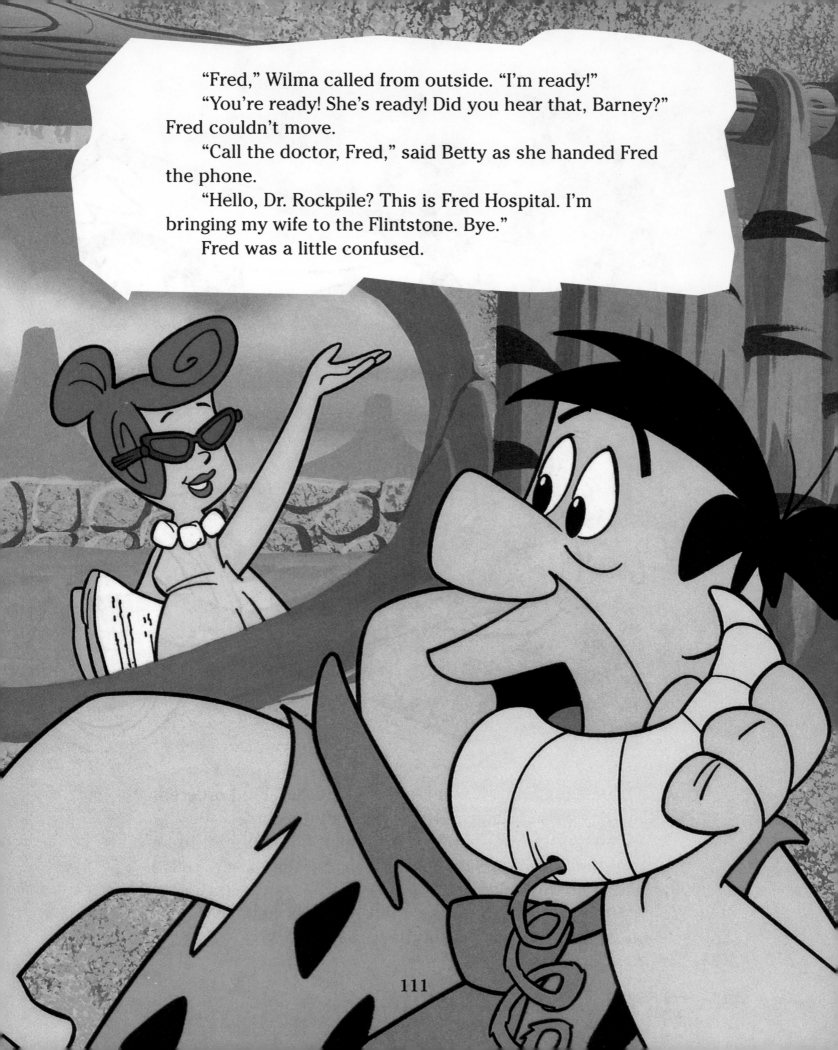

"Fred," Wilma called from outside. "I'm ready!"

"You're ready! She's ready! Did you hear that, Barney?" Fred couldn't move.

"Call the doctor, Fred," said Betty as she handed Fred the phone.

"Hello, Dr. Rockpile? This is Fred Hospital. I'm bringing my wife to the Flintstone. Bye."

Fred was a little confused.

111

"Come on, Barney, you grab the suitcase," Fred ordered. "Keep an eye on Wilma, Betty, while I get the car!"

Fred got the Flintmobile out all right, but he forgot to stop at the front door! Then he was mad when Barney yelled at him to come back.

"How can you foul things up like this, Barney?" he shouted. "Put the suitcase in the car and let's go!"

Barney tried to tell Fred that he had forgotten something.
"Not now, Barney," Fred said. "The important thing is to get Wilma to the hospital."
"But, Fred, Wilma isn't here."
"WHAT! Barney, can't you get anything straight?"

Then Barney decided he'd better drive Fred and Wilma to the hospital in his car.

"Okay, Barney," said Fred, "but I ride with Wilma."

"Right, Fred. Let's go," Barney answered.

"Where's my suitcase, Fred?" asked Wilma.

"Oh, no, Barney Rubble! You goofed again! Turn around and go back on the double!" Fred was mad now.

"The baby will be seven years old by the time we get to the hospital," Wilma said.

When they finally arrived, Fred was in charge.
"Watch your step, Wilma. Hurry up with that suitcase,
Barney."

But after Wilma went off to her room, Fred started pacing the floor of the waiting room.

"Sit down, Fred. I'll pace for you," Barney offered.

"Ahhh, thanks, Barney."

A nurse came to the door. "Mr. Flintstone? Congratulations! You're a father!"

"You mean Wilma's had the baby?" Fred jumped up. "YABBA-DABBA-DOO!"

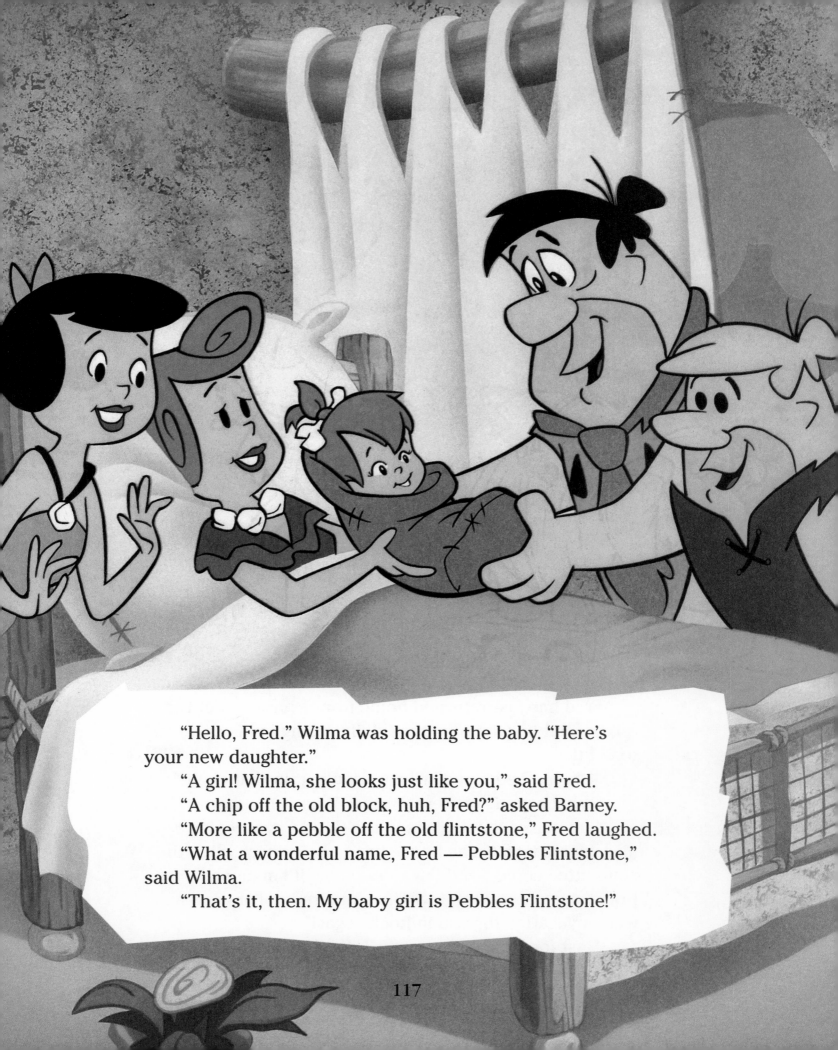

"Hello, Fred." Wilma was holding the baby. "Here's your new daughter."

"A girl! Wilma, she looks just like you," said Fred.

"A chip off the old block, huh, Fred?" asked Barney.

"More like a pebble off the old flintstone," Fred laughed.

"What a wonderful name, Fred — Pebbles Flintstone," said Wilma.

"That's it, then. My baby girl is Pebbles Flintstone!"

Operation Switchover

Fred has just returned home from a hard day at the quarry, but he won't be treated like a king in his castle tonight!

"Oh, hi, Fred," said Wilma. "Don't sit in that chair!"

"What's going on here, Wilma? What's the matter?"

"I'm one of the finalists in the Good Cavekeeping Magazine contest. The house has to be perfect when the committee comes, and I'm so nervous. If I'm named Housewife of the Year, I win five hundred dollars and a week's vacation for two in Rock Vegas!"

"Just for being a housewife?" Fred asked.

"Fred, do you think it's easy being a housewife?"

"Now, Wilma, it's just not a real job," Fred replied.

Wilma was getting very mad. "I dare you to change jobs with me for one day!"

"Are you kidding?" Fred asked. "That'll be like taking the day off!"

"All right, Fred, we'll switch. Here's my schedule for tomorrow."

119

When the alarm went off the next morning, Fred wondered why Wilma didn't get up to fix breakfast.

"I'm not cooking today, darling. Remember?" she said.

"Oh, yeah. Okay, Wilma. Breakfast coming up!"

After breakfast, Wilma put on Fred's hard hat and started for the door.

"Don't forget to cook Pebbles' cereal and feed Dino. He's growling. And you're head of the telephone committee today. It's all on the schedule. Enjoy your day off, Fred!" she said.

"I will. And don't work too hard at the quarry," Fred called after her.

Working at the quarry was not as easy as Wilma had thought!

"Drop the rocks in the pit, Wilma — the pit!"

"I'm sorry, Charlie," she called to the foreman.

But Fred was having a hard time at home, too.

"I gotta wash the dishes and bake the cake after I iron the shirts. Uh oh — I'm behind schedule — and there's the phone again!"

As the day went on, Wilma did not get better at Fred's job.
"Look out below! How was that, Charlie?"
"Go home, Mrs. Flintstone — go home!" Charlie yelled.
In the meantime Fred had made such a mess in the
house, he decided to work in the yard. That's where Barney
found him.

123

"This place looks like a disaster area, Fred!" Barney said.

"Wilma was right, Barney. Housework is harder than working at the quarry, and I'm going to tell her so."

Just then the phone rang. It was Hedda Rocker, the editor of Good Cavekeeping Magazine.

"I'll be over in twenty minutes," she said. "I'm bringing the photographer to take pictures of your house. We're close to making a decision in our contest."

Fred was frantic. There was no time to call Wilma.
"If I blow this, Wilma will kill me. We've got to get this place spotless — in twenty minutes! Barney, can you make hors d'oeuvres?"
"I don't know, Fred. What are they?"
"Those fancy little things ladies eat," Fred said.
"Sure, you can depend on me, Fred."

Hedda Rocker and Flash the photographer were very surprised when the door opened. While Fred pretended to be Wilma, Barney was in the kitchen making hors d'oeuvres out of whatever he could find.

"Ah, here's a can of Dino's food. I'll just add some mustard and cactus salt," he said to himself.

As soon as the hors d'oeuvres were ready, Fred brought them into the living room.

"I don't know how you do it, Wilma. These are delicious," said Hedda. "As Housewife of the Year, you'll have to share the recipe."

"You mean Wilma wins? I mean — I win?" Fred asked.

"Of course. This house is spotless!" Hedda said.

"YABBA-DABBA-DOO!" yelled Fred.

127

The next morning Fred was happy to serve Wilma her breakfast in bed.

"Nothing is too good for the Housewife of the Year!" he told her.

"I'm glad the people at Good Cavekeeping could laugh about your trick, Fred. And now that I know how tough your job is, I'm happy with mine. Let me get your breakfast now, dear."

"We're lucky, you know it, Wilma?"

DROOPY™
RANGER DROOPY TO THE RESCUE

Written by Ronald Kidd
Art by John Kurtz

Times were hard in the little town of Tumbleweed. They'd been that way ever since Wolfie Joe arrived. He was the meanest, lowest, nastiest critter west of the Pecos.

Joe lived in a little shack outside of town. Every afternoon he would jump on his horse and come galloping through Tumbleweed, whooping and hollering and shooting to beat the band.

131

As you can imagine, people hated it. It got to where they wouldn't even go outside for fear of Wolfie Joe. Business dropped off, and the place started looking like a ghost town.

You might ask what the sheriff was doing all this time. Well, you see, that was part of the problem.

There was no sheriff.

Wolfie Joe had run him out of town, and the one after that, and the one after that. So many sheriffs got chased off that, according to legend, they started a little town of their own, called Sheriffs Town.

BULLET TIN BOARD

WANTED

HELP! SHERIFF WANTED NOW!

There was a mayor in Tumbleweed, though. He wasn't the bravest fellow in the world, but he was smart enough to know when he was in trouble. And in those days, when you were in trouble you called the Texas Rangers.

He sent off a telegram and waited. Before long, the reply came back. The Rangers would send out their best man on the next stagecoach.

That night, Wolfie Joe read all about it in the paper. It seemed that the mayor had announced a big celebration to welcome the Texas Ranger, and the whole town would be there.

Joe chuckled to himself. He'd be there, *too*, to give this hotshot Ranger a little greeting of his own.

The town was hopping the next day. There were banners, a brass band, and lots of happy faces. At the back of the crowd, lurking in the shadows, was Wolfie Joe.

At noon the stagecoach arrived in a cloud of dust. When the air cleared, the door opened, and a lone figure stepped out.

It was Ranger Droopy.

"Hello, everybody," he said in a small, sad voice.

Wolfie Joe started to laugh so loud the ground shook. And he kept on laughing during the music and the speeches and the special presentations.

Then he stopped, because it's hard to laugh when your eyes are popping out of your head. You see, Miss Tumbleweed had just walked out on stage.

Let me tell you, folks, she was something
to behold. She stepped up to Ranger Droopy,
handed him a bouquet of flowers, and planted
a big kiss right on his forehead.
"Yippee-oh-ki-ay," Droopy commented.

Well, sir, Wolfie Joe had seen enough. As Miss Tumbleweed walked Ranger Droopy to his hotel, Joe sneaked up from behind and gave Droopy a big push. Droopy landed facedown in a puddle. When he looked up, he was dripping with mud.

"You know what?" said Droopy. "That makes me mad."

Wolfie Joe roared with laughter. "I'll be back, darlin'," he
crowed, as he winked at Miss Tumbleweed. "You ain't seen
the last of me!"

Then he jumped on his horse and went riding out of town.

Well, the townsfolk couldn't stop talking about it. Wolfie Joe
had threatened a Texas Ranger and had apparently gotten the
better of him. Could he do it again?
   The future of the town was at stake, not to mention the
future of Miss Tumbleweed.

That night, while Wolfie Joe slept, Droopy tiptoed into his shack, stayed for a few minutes, and tiptoed out again. Droopy had a surprise in store for Wolfie Joe.

145

Joe rode into town as usual the next afternoon.
Seeing Miss Tumbleweed, he decided to put on
a little show for her. He whooped and hollered, and
just as he was about to start shooting up the place,
Ranger Droopy stepped out of the hotel.

"Stop, or you'll be sorry," Droopy mumbled.

146

Wolfie Joe grinned at Miss Tumbleweed, took out his gun, and pulled the trigger.

Water squirted out, to Joe's surprise. He looked pretty embarrassed.

"I told you you'd be sorry," said Droopy, who had a few tricks up his sleeve.

Picking up a fire hose, Ranger Droopy nodded at one of his deputies to turn on the water full force. Droopy blasted Joe out of his saddle and hosed him right out of town.

149

Wolfie Joe bought a new gun and came riding back the next day. He headed straight to the hotel and stepped inside. The lobby was empty except for a jar in the middle of the floor.

"Why is everything so quiet?" he bellowed.

"It's not quiet," said a quiet voice. "The place is buzzing."

The voice belonged to Ranger Droopy, who was
hiding in the hallway. He pulled a string, and out of the
jar came a swarm of angry bees. They chased Joe around the
lobby a few times, then through the door and down the street.

151

You can bet that Wolfie Joe was back the next day. He was all set to stage the biggest shoot-em-up the town had ever seen when he saw a sign. It read...

Arm-Wrestling Contest

and first prize was a kiss from Miss Tumbleweed!
     Wolfie Joe chuckled. By entering the contest, he could beat Ranger Droopy *and* win Miss Tumbleweed in the bargain!

The contest started. Arm wrestlers
stepped up, one after the other, to
challenge Wolfie Joe. They stepped down
just as fast.

Before long, it was Ranger Droopy's turn.
When he shuffled forward, the crowd held its
breath. Droopy had shown a lot of bravery
for a little fellow, but was he really
stronger than Wolfie Joe?

Well, the truth was sure and
simple.
 The match was over in a
heartbeat, and Ranger Droopy
was on the losing end.

"Now, how about a kiss?" said Wolfie Joe, grinning at Miss Tumbleweed. She tried stepping away, but Wolfie Joe just moved in closer.

Ranger Droopy interrupted just in time. "Pardon me, but I think there's one more contestant," he said.

Droopy motioned, and an old woman came out of the hotel.

"Mom!" gulped Wolfie Joe. "What are you doing here?"

"Ranger Droopy sent for me. Now, give me that arm." She was so strong that folks thought there was an earthquake when Wolfie Joe's arm hit the ground.

Then she grabbed him by the ear and led him away in a hurry. "What's all this I hear about you causing trouble?" she hollered. "It's about time you learned some manners."

The crowd roared with laughter and cheered with joy. The mayor was so happy, he asked Droopy if he'd like to stay on to be the sheriff. Droopy accepted, and right then Miss Tumbleweed gave him a big kiss.

Droopy hadn't really won the contest, but nobody seemed to mind.

These days, Wolfie Joe still comes to town every afternoon. But now it's with his mom. Turns out that Joe's quite handy when it comes to bagging groceries.

And Droopy? He's still the sheriff, and his wife's real proud of him. She used to be Miss Tumbleweed, but now they call her Mrs. Droopy.

Their kids are proud, too. And judging from the looks of them, Tumbleweed won't have any more trouble finding sheriffs.

SCOOBY-DOO™

Story Adaptations by Etta Wilson

Illustrations by Bob Singer

Art Direction by Linda Karl

161

What a Night For a Knight

Scooby-Doo and his friends Shaggy, Velma, Daphne, and Freddy were walking home from the movie. The moon was full and it was a nervous night! Suddenly they spotted a pickup truck sitting in the road ahead.

"Rhut's rat?" barked Scooby.

"Look! There's an empty old suit of black armor in the driver's seat," said Freddy.

"Maybe he went out for the night! Get it?" Shaggy's joke didn't seem too funny to anybody but Scooby. There was a tag on a large crate in the back of the truck. It said:

Professor J. Hyde-White, Archaeologist
London, England
Deliver to the County Museum

"So that's where this knight was headed for," Velma said.

"Yes, but where's the professor?" asked Daphne.

"Looks like another mystery to solve!"

"Right!" said Scooby.

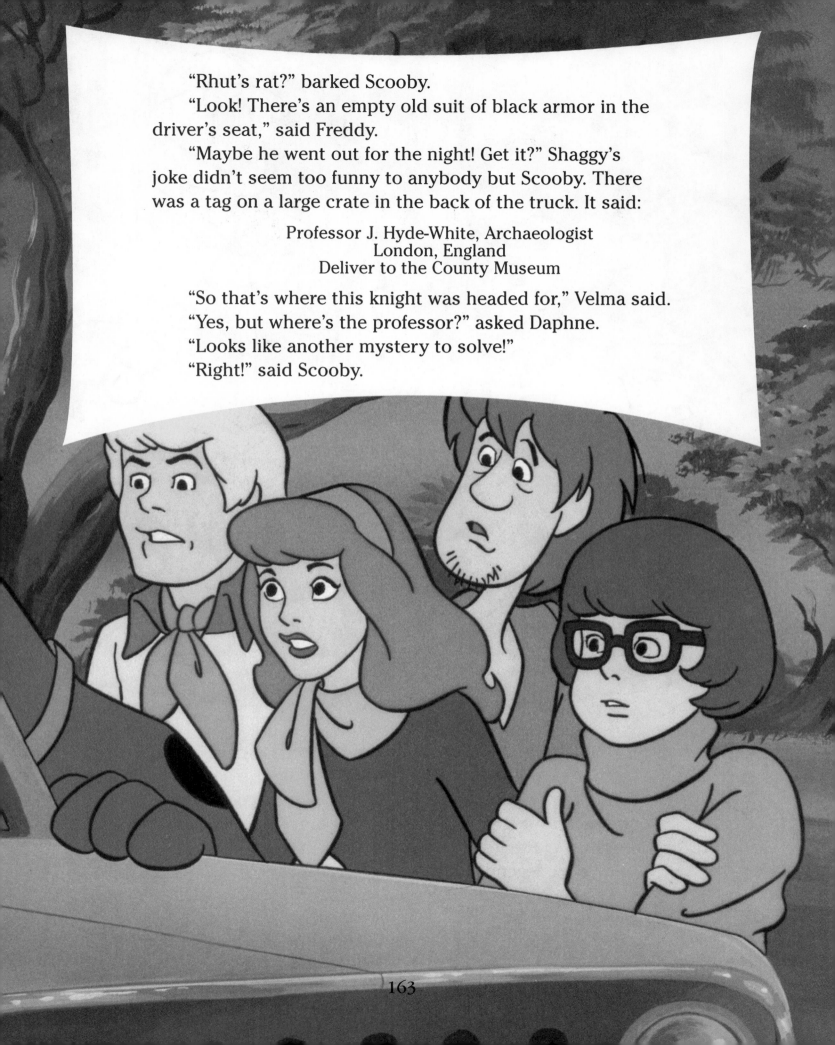

163

They started looking for clues at the museum. The man in charge, Mr. Wikles, didn't seem very happy that they had found the Black Knight. He said it was not a good time for the professor to be delivering the armor from England — because of the legend.

"What legend?" asked Freddy.

"The Black Knight is supposed to come alive when the moon is full."

"Wow! The moon was full last night!" said Shaggy.

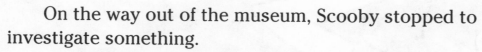

On the way out of the museum, Scooby stopped to investigate something.

"Scooby-Doo, where are you?" called Daphne.

Scooby barked and ran to catch up. He was wearing some strange glasses, and no one knew what they were.

"There's one way to find out!" said Freddy.

At the library they read that the special glasses were used by archaeologists and were only made in England. Now they were sure something fishy was going on at the museum.

That night they went back to the museum. It was locked up tighter than a drum, but thin-man Shaggy found a way in — with help from a ladder and a jack.

Once they were all inside, they decided to split up to look for the professor.

"You stand guard, Scooby," said Freddy.

"Uh-uh . . . Uh-uh!" Scooby didn't want to be alone in the dark museum.

"Would you do it for a Scooby Snack?" Freddy asked.

Scooby couldn't say no! "Slurp, chomp, gulp!"

Velma and Shaggy hadn't gone far before they realized they were being followed — by Scooby! The three of them started through the dark rooms. Shaggy pulled the shade on the window to keep out the bright moon. Then he took a wrong turn!

"Oh, no! We lost Shaggy," cried Velma.

Scooby's teeth began to chatter.

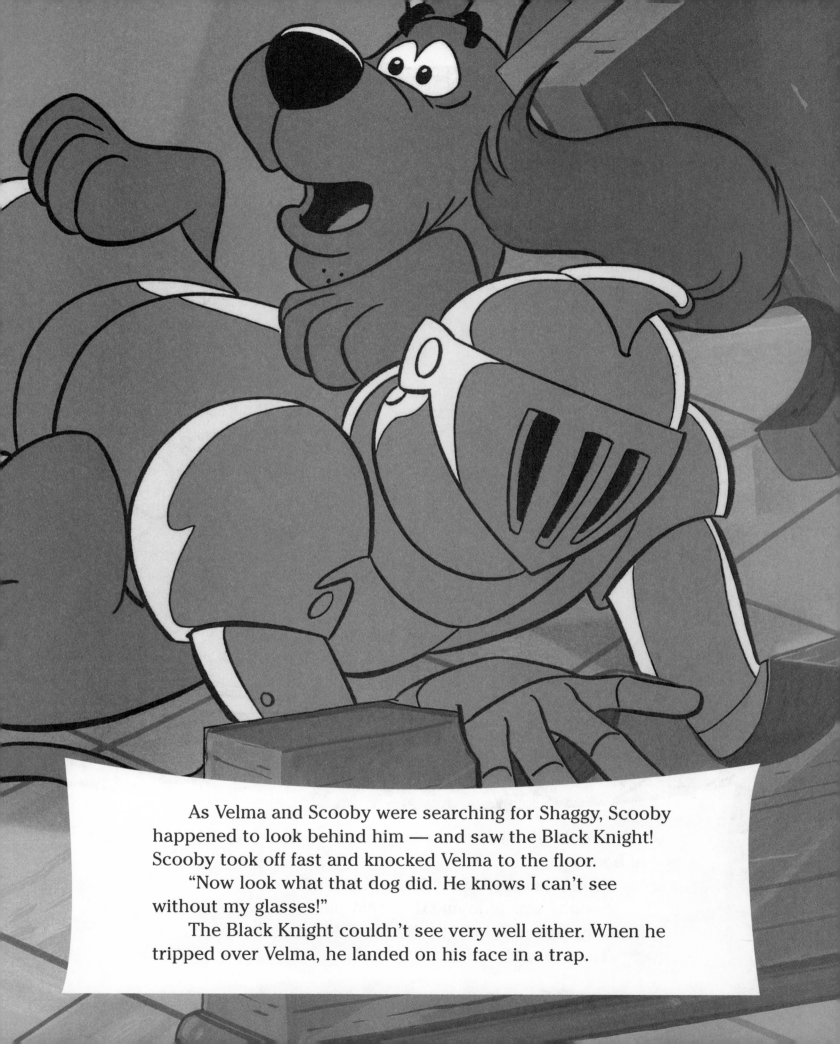

As Velma and Scooby were searching for Shaggy, Scooby happened to look behind him — and saw the Black Knight! Scooby took off fast and knocked Velma to the floor.

"Now look what that dog did. He knows I can't see without my glasses!"

The Black Knight couldn't see very well either. When he tripped over Velma, he landed on his face in a trap.

Scooby had found the best room of all. It was full of bones!

"Sniff. Scooby-Dooby-Doo . . . Slurp!"

Scooby was enjoying the great pile of bones until he heard moans. He thought the Black Knight had found him. Time to run!

In the gallery Shaggy noticed a picture missing from the wall. He was sure the Black Knight was walking around just as the legend said, and called everyone to help him check the clue. Then Daphne found something else.

"Is that blood on the floor?" she asked.

"No, it's paint — and it leads down the hall," said Freddy.

The trail of paint ended at the mummy case. And behind the case was a secret room! It was very messy with lots of paintings, some of them only half-done.

"Look! There are two paintings exactly alike!"

"Right, Velma," said Freddy. "This just about solves the mystery!"

"Rit does???" barked Scooby.

They started out the back to call the sheriff, but Daphne picked the wrong door. Time to run again!

In the relic room, Shaggy and Scooby hid in an old biplane. When the plane started, Scooby decided to be the pilot, and the chase was on. Now it was the Black Knight who was running away!

The plane caught him. As the Knight's helmet fell off, they saw he was not a knight at all.

It was Mr. Wikles!

The sheriff arrived, and Freddy, Velma, Shaggy, and Daphne put all the clues together. Mr. Wikles was part of a gang who stole the real paintings from the museum and put up fake ones. They had to get rid of the professor because he would have spotted the fakes.

"Oh, my gosh!" said Daphne. "We never found Professor Hyde-White."

"Rook! Rook!" Scooby barked.

"It's Scooby-Doo with a shoe!" said Velma.

Scooby led them straight to the Professor. He was explaining how Wikles had made up the legend about the Black Knight — when they saw the suit of armor move!

"Zoinks! He's alive!" exclaimed Shaggy.

But it was Scooby having the last laugh on his friends. "Scooby-Dooby-Doo!"

Scooby Gumbo

It's Mardi Gras time in New Orleans. Shaggy, Scooby,
and Scrappy are having a great time marching in the parade.

"This is great Dixieland jazz, eh, guys?" Shaggy asked.

"Reah, Razz!" barked Scooby.

"Hey, Uncle Scooby, look up there." Scrappy had spotted a French restaurant on the street ahead.

"Like, New Orleans seafood . . . sounds good to me," said Shaggy.

"Right!" Scooby was all for eating.

179

At the table on the sidewalk, they were greeted by the French chef.

"Bonjour. Your order please?" Then he took a close look at Scooby and Scrappy. "We do not serve zee dogs zere!" he said.

"Rogs? Rhere?" asked Scooby.

"Oud! Get oud!" the chef roared and kicked all three of them out of the restaurant.

"You big meanie!" yelled Scrappy. "You can't do that to my Uncle Scooby. Let's go back in there and eat!"

180

"Raggy, rook!" Scooby saw something very interesting across the street — a wig shop.

"Hey, Scrappy, come on," called Shaggy. "I've got an idea. Where's there a wig, there's a way!"

Soon they were back at the restaurant, looking very different.

"Give us three orders of shrimp creole," ordered Shaggy.

"As you wish, monsieur," said the chef. He started for the kitchen without a word about not serving dogs. The wigs had worked!

"Hey, I wonder what this thing does." Scrappy pulled on the arm of a diving suit beside the door. When the suit made a growling noise, Scrappy was ready to fight!

"Rappy-Roo!" barked Scooby.

"Don't worry, Uncle Scooby. I can handle him!"

Scrappy twisted the helmet of the suit so hard, it flew through the air — right onto the chef's head as he came from the kitchen!

"Someone will pay for zis!" he yelled.

"Zoinks! Like, run!" called Shaggy.

They found a place to hide on a float in the parade, but the chef was right behind them.

"Dogs! There you are! I'll get you!" he shouted as he climbed onto the float.

SEA FOOD

RESTA

The three friends slipped into a band on the sidewalk. Scooby played the biggest instrument in the band — and tried to hide at the same time.

"Let's make it snappy, Scoob. Get it?" laughed Shaggy.

"Reah!"

"Gotcha!" The chef had found them and he was very mad! "Zere ees no place to hide!"

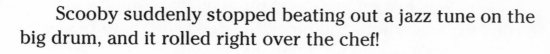

Scooby suddenly stopped beating out a jazz tune on the big drum, and it rolled right over the chef!

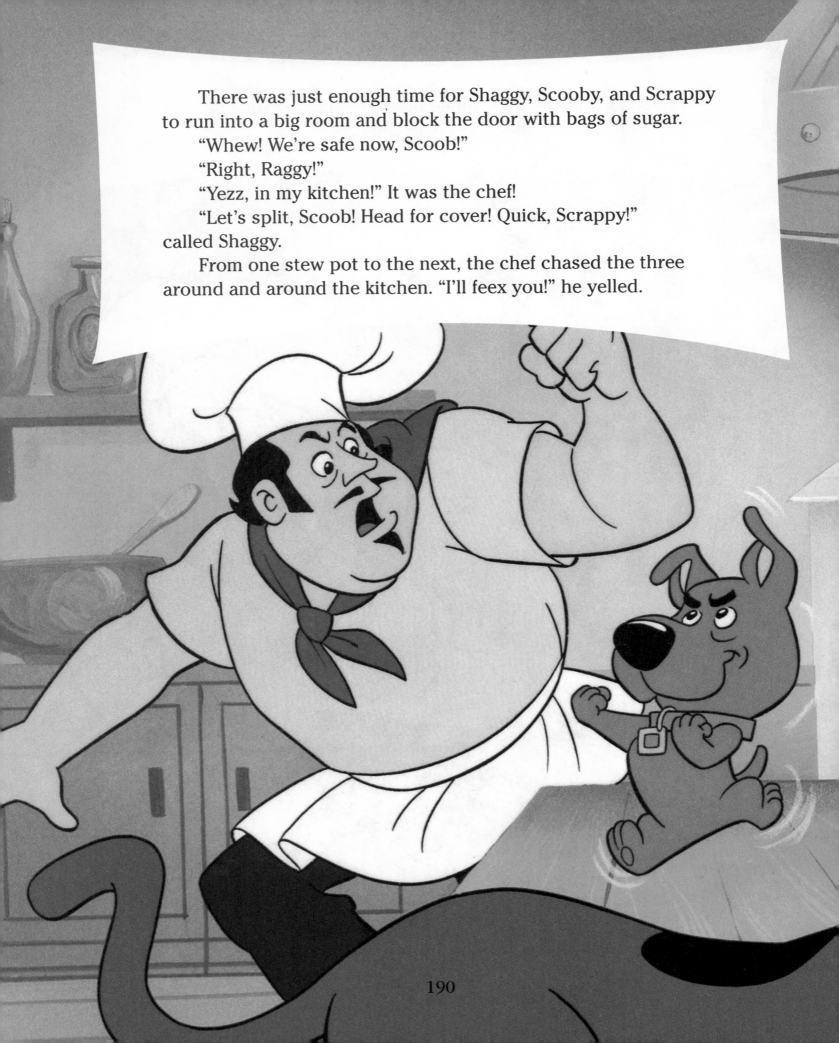

There was just enough time for Shaggy, Scooby, and Scrappy to run into a big room and block the door with bags of sugar.

"Whew! We're safe now, Scoob!"

"Right, Raggy!"

"Yezz, in my kitchen!" It was the chef!

"Let's split, Scoob! Head for cover! Quick, Scrappy!" called Shaggy.

From one stew pot to the next, the chef chased the three around and around the kitchen. "I'll feex you!" he yelled.

Then Scrappy found the mixer.

"I'll fix that mean old chef with a batch of my special sticky, scrappy gumbo!"

He poured some of everything on the counter into the mixing bowl and flipped the switch. The gumbo was ready to serve just as the chef slipped on a pile of sugar beside the counter!

"Slurp! Slurp! What is zis?" The chef liked what he tasted. "This gives me an idea! I still do not allow dogs in my restaurant, but zey are welcome in my kitchen!"

"Ruh?" asked Scooby.

A short while later everyone was busy in the kitchen.
"Okay, Uncle Scooby, I'm ready to decorate the cupcakes
we baked," Scrappy called. But he iced Scooby's face!
"That Scrappy is some pastry chef, Scoob, but it looks
like you're for dessert." Shaggy laughed.
"Reah, slurp, slurp. Scooby-Dooby-Doo!"

Scooby Doo Finds the Clue

ROCKY POINT BEACH

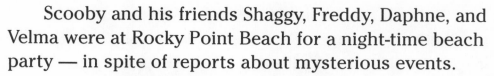

Scooby and his friends Shaggy, Freddy, Daphne, and Velma were at Rocky Point Beach for a night-time beach party — in spite of reports about mysterious events.

"Wow! I can already taste those chocolate-covered hot dogs!" said Shaggy.

"Yuck! Your stomach must be made of scrap iron," Velma replied.

"Where is Scooby-Doo?" Freddy asked. "I haven't seen him since we unloaded the Mystery Machine."

"He went surfing," said Daphne as they danced.

Out on the surfboard, Scooby had bumped into something strange. "Ripes!" barked Scooby.
"Zoinks!" yelled Shaggy. "It's a seagoing ghost!!"

196

The whole gang ran up the beach to hide behind some rocks. Scooby ran the fastest!

"There's something mighty spooky going on here," said Daphne.

"Right!" Velma said. "The newspaper reported that boats vanish on this beach and the sheriff can't find them."

"Maybe the old beach hermit, Ebenezer Shark, can give us a clue. Let's pay him a visit — tonight," said Freddy.

Ebenezer Shark was sure that Scooby and his friends had seen the ghost of Captain Cutler.

"How do you know it was Captain Cutler?" Freddy asked.

"Because his boat was wrecked on a foggy night like this. It ran into one of those fancy yachts and sent Captain Cutler down to the graveyard of ships. But his ghost always moves through the fog just before the boats vanish."

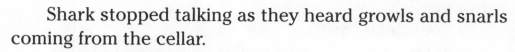

Shark stopped talking as they heard growls and snarls coming from the cellar.

"Hey, it's Scooby," said Daphne.

"Zoinks! He's got that ghost again!" Shaggy yelled.

"Oh, no," said Shark, "that's my old diving suit. Now if you want to know more about Cutler, you'd better see his wife up at the old lighthouse."

"Ol righthouse?" Scooby gulped.

Velma, Shaggy, and Scooby went inside the creepy lighthouse.

"It looks like she practices witchcraft," said Velma.

Just then Shaggy felt long skinny fingers on his shoulder. It was widow Cutler.

"We think we saw the ghost of Captain Cutler tonight," Velma said to the old woman.

"Aye, you did," she replied. "I brought him back from the grave with my witchcraft, but I should have left him under the sea. Now he's made another yacht vanish to get revenge for his wreck."

"Let's get out of this scary pad," Shaggy whispered to Velma.

MAGIC
MADE EASY

Out on the beach, they saw a strange glow coming from a drain pipe. Velma and Shaggy pushed Scooby in to investigate. In minutes he was back with his mouth full.

"Like, wow! Glowing seaweed!" said Shaggy.

"That seaweed is found only in the graveyard of ships below the water," Velma said. "That's where Captain Cutler went down and that's where we'll find the answer to our mystery!"

"Well, Scooby-Dooby-Doo!" barked Scooby.

Scooby and the gang dressed in scuba diving suits. Soon they were on a boat headed out to sea.

"Look, there's one of the yachts from the marina," said Daphne. "And it's moving toward that cove."

"But there's no one on board," Freddy pointed out.

"What's making it go?" asked Freddy.

"Ghost power!" Velma replied.

"Well, like I always say — onward and downward — to the graveyard of ships, that is," said Freddy.

When they dived below the water, they split into two teams to look for the ghost. Shaggy and Scooby swam toward one of the old sunken ships. They didn't know they were being watched.

"Raggy, rook!" barked Scooby. He had found glowing footprints on the ocean floor.

"Okay, Scoob, let's follow them inside the ship, but back-to-back so we don't get surprised!" said Shaggy.

In the dark cabin of the ship it was hard to see.
"Scooby-Doo, Scooby-Doo, where are you?" called
Shaggy.
"I found a rue, Raggy! I found a rue!"
"A clue, Scooby? Zoinks! It's scuba tanks — all ready for
use! Let's find the gang quick."

Shaggy and Scooby swam out to tell Freddy, Daphne, and Velma about the scuba tanks. Then Daphne spotted more glowing footprints.

"Those footprints vanish right into the side of the cliff," said Velma. "Now what do we do?"

"Like, rest — I'm pooped!" Shaggy sat on a nearby rock. Suddenly a door in the cliff opened to a secret passage.

"Shaggy, you're a genius!" Freddy said. "Come on gang, let's follow his trail."

At the end of the secret passage, Scooby and the gang found a giant hidden cavern full of yachts.

"Look, there's the yacht we saw disappear in the cove, and it's tied to a mini-sub," said Daphne.

"Things are beginning to add up," Freddy said. "And I've got a plan."

He put a bar of soap in a spray container, attached it to a fire hose on one of the boats, and turned on the water. Instant suds!

"Okay, Shaggy, start the noisemaker."

When the ghost came down the ramp, he slipped in the suds and fell right into Scooby's net. The glowing ghost was trapped.

"Now let's see who our mystery ghost is," said Freddy. Velma pulled off the helmet. Who is it?" she asked.

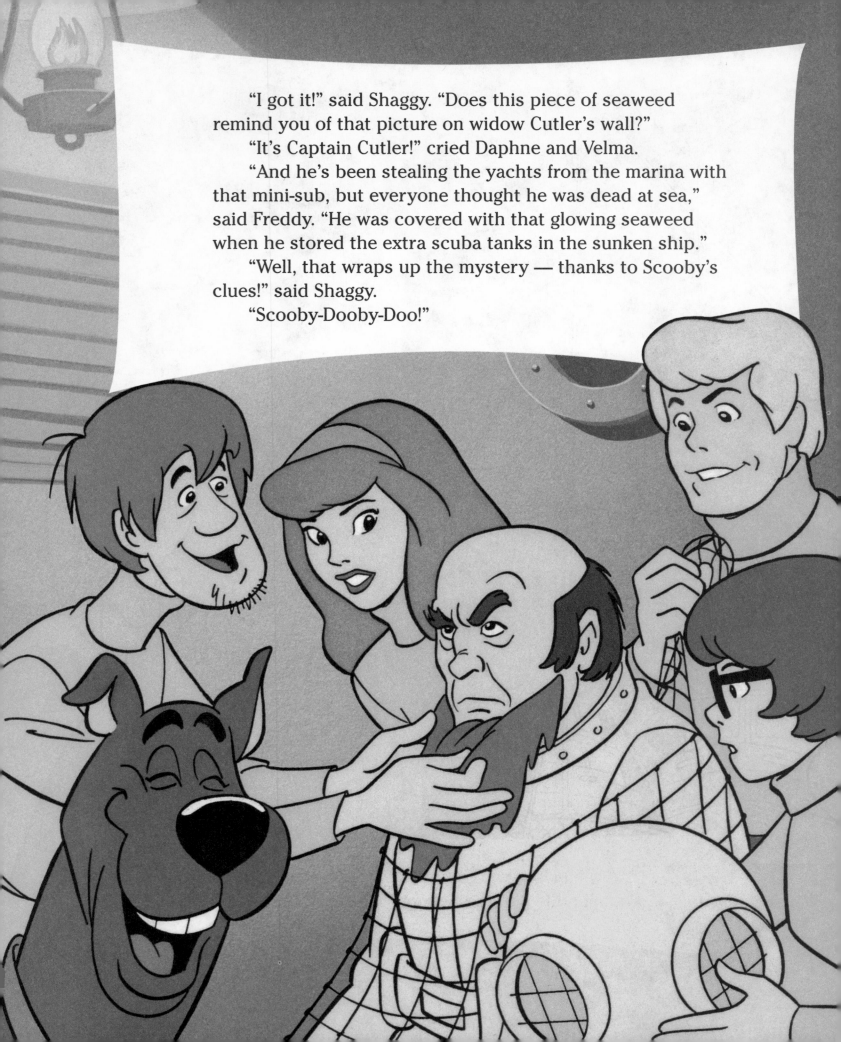

"I got it!" said Shaggy. "Does this piece of seaweed remind you of that picture on widow Cutler's wall?"

"It's Captain Cutler!" cried Daphne and Velma.

"And he's been stealing the yachts from the marina with that mini-sub, but everyone thought he was dead at sea," said Freddy. "He was covered with that glowing seaweed when he stored the extra scuba tanks in the sunken ship."

"Well, that wraps up the mystery — thanks to Scooby's clues!" said Shaggy.

"Scooby-Dooby-Doo!"

TOM and JERRY™
SKATE, RATTLE AND ROLL

Written by Ronald Kidd
Paintings by H. R. Russell

See that guy? No, not the goldfish, the one with the whiskers and the sneaky look on his face. The one who likes to tease small animals–like fish and mice, for example.

Yes, that's the one. His name is Tom, and boy, is he about to get a surprise.

YIKES!

Tom thinks he sees a scary monster in the goldfish bowl.

He can't understand what's going on. After all, it's Tom who is supposed to do the scaring around here.

What's really going on is a trick.

See, it wasn't a monster at all. It was Jerry, the mouse that Tom chases constantly. He's just a little guy, but the glass bowl made his face look huge and ugly. Now Jerry's laughing his head off.

The bad part for Jerry is that Tom just figured the whole thing out. And...

The chase is on—again.

Sometimes Tom catches Jerry, but the speedy mouse usually manages to get away. Jerry has had some *very close* calls, though.

Suddenly, Tom has Jerry in his paw, and it looks like there's no way out. As Tom starts to squeeze Jerry, he gets a big squirt of water right in the face.

Splash! Tom lets go, and just like that, Jerry's home free.

Tom and Jerry have been doing this for years. They figure it's always going to be this way.

But one day, something happens that changes everything.

215

Mrs. McNulty, Tom's owner, has a surprise guest for Tom.

"Tom, there's someone very special I'd like you to meet," she says. Jerry can't imagine who this might be.

Tom is quite surprised to see a very pretty little girl come into the room.

"This is Clara, my niece," says Mrs. McNulty. "She'll be staying with us for a few days. I think you two will have a nice time playing together. Don't you, Tom?"

Tom nods his head and smiles his sweetest smile.

"I'll be right in the next room. Have fun, you two," Mrs. NcNulty says.

As soon as she's gone, Jerry decides to introduce himself. After all, he figures he's a lot sweeter than Tom is, and he would like to play too.

Jerry steps out in Clara's view and takes a bow. Ta-da! Clara doesn't say hello. She just starts screaming at the top of her lungs! In a flash Mrs. McNulty is back and begins to chase Jerry around the house with a broom.

This just doesn't seem fair to poor Jerry.

Clara quickly forgets about Jerry and goes right back to playing with Tom. "You're my poopsie-woopsie, huggy-wuggy, most lovable kitty-cat in the whole wide world," she says, hugging him tightly.

Clara gets a ball of yarn and starts tossing it to Tom. Every time he catches it, she jumps up and down, clapping.

"Good kitty! Good kitty!" she cries.

Clara thinks Tom is one very sweet cat.

Too bad she doesn't stick around to
see what her good kitty does next.
As soon as she leaves the room,
Tom uses the yarn to make a lasso,
then ropes Jerry and reels him in.

Luckily Jerry wriggles out, or
he might have ended up as part
of a cat food casserole.

The next day, Clara comes looking for Tom again.

"Let's play dolls!" she says.

Tom notices doll clothes but no doll. Then, before he knows what hit him, Clara pins a diaper around him and ties a bonnet on his head.

"My sweet baby, time to eat," she says as she pops a bottle in his mouth.

222

Jerry thinks it's great! Especially since Clara left the bottle out where Jerry could get at it. **Squirt!**—Tom gets a big mouthful sprayed right at him.

The next day, things get even worse for Tom. It seems Clara wants to play cops and robbers, and Tom is the robber.

"Hands up, mister," she tells Tom. "You're going to jail!"

Clara marches Tom over to a big, empty
bird cage and shuts him inside. When
she turns her back, Jerry snaps a lock
on the door.

"Now, how did that happen?"
Clara wonders as she goes off
to look for the key.

225

Jerry slips out from his hiding place and flashes Tom a big grin. Tom is angry now. He lunges at Jerry but manages only to bump his head on the bars.

Next, Jerry does a little dance around the cage, just out of Tom's reach. This *really* drives Tom crazy!

226

Then comes the big finale. Jerry opens a can of tuna, Tom's favorite food, and nibbles on it, licking his fingers one by one. Tom's eyes get big and he starts to drool. By the time Clara gets back, the bottom of the cage is like a big lake.

"Bad kitty!" she says. "Just for that, you'll have to stay in there until tomorrow!"

Tom doesn't get much sleep that night, so when Clara lets him out the next morning, he can barely keep his eyes open.

"Today we're going to have lots of fun," she says. "We're going roller skating!"

She takes Tom outside, straps him into a pair of skates, and gives him a push right down a great big hill.

"Whee!" she says, and off Tom goes.

Tom starts off slowly. Then he begins to pick up speed. He rolls down the driveway and onto the sidewalk. Pretty soon Tom's zooming along, passing cars and trucks! He thinks that this could be the end of him.

231

Luckily for Tom, there's a
hedge at the bottom of the hill, and
that's *exactly* where he lands.

   Jerry catches up with him a minute later, and he's
shocked. But it's not because of the way Tom looks.

   Jerry actually feels sorry for Tom.

   Clara doesn't seem to notice what bad shape her
playmate is in.

Clara picks up Tom and begins carrying him back to the house. "It'll be even more fun tomorrow. We're having a tea party!" she says.

As Jerry watches them climb the hill, he starts thinking. His thoughts turn into an idea, and the idea becomes a plan to save his friend.

The next day, Clara comes skipping into the room and announces, "Tea party time!"

She gets out a teapot and teacups and sits her dolls at the table. She dresses Tom in a frilly pink outfit and takes him into the kitchen to get some cookies. When she brings the cookies back, the dolls have sprouted mustaches!

"My babies!" she cries. "How did this happen to you?"

She sets the cookies down and tries to rub off the mustaches. When she looks back a moment later, the cookies are gone! There's nothing left but a few crumbs.

"My cookies!" she cries. "Who has eaten them?"

235

Just then, the teapot starts shaking. It tips one way, then another, and it starts wobbling across the table.

"My teapot!" she shrieks. "What's wrong with it?"

The teapot comes to a stop.

"Thank goodness!" she says. "Now we can continue our tea party."

Without warning the top pops off, and a mouse jumps out! It's Jerry to the rescue!

Clara leaps from her seat and runs out of the room, down the stairs and through the door. Tom and Jerry are certain she won't be coming back.

Tom stands by the door, staring in amazement.
Clara is gone for good! For the first time in days,
Tom is grinning!

In a flash, he charges after Jerry, tearing off his tea party outfit piece by piece.

Once again Jerry is running for his life, just like the good old days! The two friends are at it again, better than ever before.

THE Jetsons™

Story Adaptations by Etta Wilson
Illustrations by Bob Singer
Art Direction by Linda Karl

241

Introducing Astro

Jane Jetson greeted Judy and Elroy, who just came home from school. Elroy wasn't alone, though—he had a friend. "Mom! Guess who came home with me?!"

"My goodness, what is this? A monster?" shouted Jane in surprise.

"It's not a monster, Mom. His name is Astro and he's just a little puppy. Can I keep him? Please? Can I?"

"Mom, please let us keep him! He's so cute," Judy begged.

"You kids know your dad doesn't like dogs . . . oh, all right, I'll call his office and ask," Jane promised.

When Jane appeared on George's television phone, she interrupted another productive day. As always, George was busy pushing buttons at Spacely Sprockets.

"I have a big favor to ask you, darling," Jane began. "We want a dog."

"No—not again. I've told you hundreds of times. There's no room in our house for a dog. The answer is no!"

George knew the whole family was sore at him when the television phone suddenly went blank.

"Shee! If I don't get a dog, I'll be in the dog house! I'd better use the computer to figure out this one."

"And the answer is . . . of course! We'll get an apartment-approved electronic dog!"

LECTRONIMO

Jane, Judy, and Elroy welcomed George home with big grins on their faces. That was part of their plan. They were hoping to keep Astro. But George had a surprise for them—Lectronimo!

"Gee, Dad!" shouted Elroy. "What's that? We already have a vacuum cleaner!"

Then George noticed Astro, the puppy. George was less than thrilled by Elroy's new dog.

"That's a dog? Looks more like a giraffe! Get it out of here! Now!"

Judy had an idea. "Let's have a contest between Lectronimo and Astro."

"Yeah, the best dog stays!" said Elroy.

"I'll be scorekeeper, and there'll be no favorites," George told them.

FETCHING	1	0
ROLLING OVER	1	0
OVER-EATING	0	1
OBEYING COMMANDS	1	0
BRINGING SLIPPERS	1	0
TOTAL	4	1

First Astro raced Lectronimo to find a bone and then to bring George's slippers. No matter what the contest called for, Lectronimo was too fast every time. Astro lost.

George agreed to let Astro stay for the night, but tomorrow he was out!

"Good night, Astro," sniffed Elroy.

The Jetsons—and Astro—were sound asleep when the cat burglar opened the window.

"I'll clean out the place and be gone before—"

BARK! BARK! BARK!

"Oh, no, it's one of them nuclear-powered dogs! Help! Help!"

George heard the commotion and got up to see what was going on. He ran right into the burglar—or rather, the burglar ran right into him.

"Hey, what's this? Who are you?" George asked.

"Here, buddy," said the burglar, "put this mask on."

"Bark, bark, bark!"

"Good puppy, Lectronimo! Grab him!" George shouted.

"Bark, bark, bark!"

"Not me! I'm not the burglar! Help!"

"Don't worry, Dad!" Elroy decided to give his puppy a chance to prove himself.

"Hey, Astro! Wake up! There's a burglar in the house!"

Hearing the word "burglar," Astro got up and ran—in the opposite direction! Meanwhile, the burglar was running as fast as his legs would carry him to get away from Lectronimo. When suddenly: BAM!

"Wheee! He did it!" Elroy shouted. "Astro caught the burglar!"

When Jane and Judy woke up, George stood at the door—accompanied by a policeman.

"Ladies, this masked bandit was breaking into your home," said the policeman.

"But, officer, this is my husband," Jane said. "This electronic dog mistook him for a burglar."

"That's right! And my dog, Astro, caught the real burglar!" Elroy boasted.

"All right. All right," said George. "But I hope he doesn't think he's the only hero around here!"

257

The Flying Suit

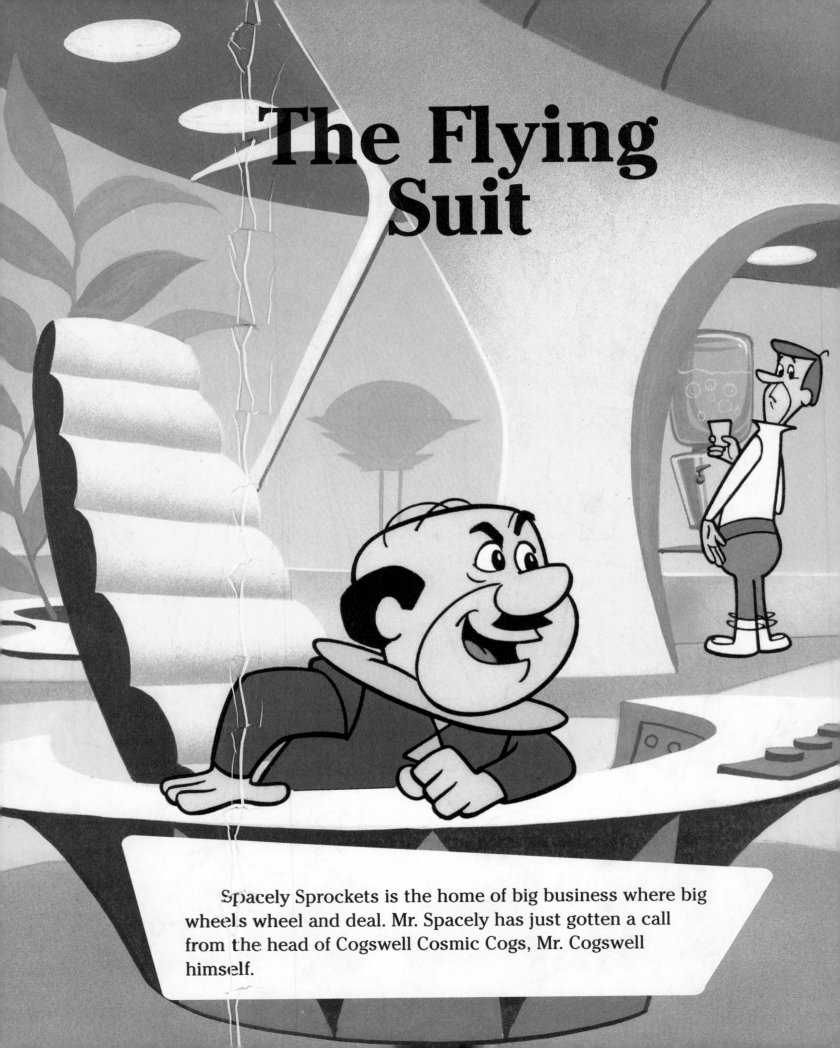

Spacely Sprockets is the home of big business where big wheels wheel and deal. Mr. Spacely has just gotten a call from the head of Cogswell Cosmic Cogs, Mr. Cogswell himself.

"Hi there, Spacely. Did you accept my offer? When do we merge?" Cogswell asked.

"The first Sunday that comes in the middle of the week! You can't take over Spacely Sprockets, Cogswell. You're bluffing!"

"Not at all, Spacely! Our research boys have a big new breakthrough. You'd better sell out now."

"Don't hold your breath!" Spacely yelled.

Back at Cogswell Cosmic Cogs, it was time to test the great new breakthrough—a flying suit!

"Why, it looks like an ordinary suit! Is this a gag, Moonstone?" asked Cogswell.

"Oh, no, Mr. Cogswell! With this suit on, Harlan can fly like a bird! The X-1500 flying suit obeys the slightest command of anyone who wears it."

"Fantastic, Moonstone! We're geniuses! Now take the suit to the cleaners. We want it looking fresh for the Board of Directors meeting tomorrow."

"Hey, Herb, I need a rush job on this suit," Harlan said to the man at the cleaners.

"Sure thing. It only takes fifteen seconds with the new high speed sound waves."

"Great! I'll be right back for it."

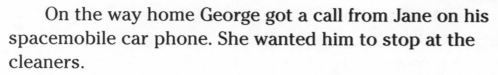

On the way home George got a call from Jane on his spacemobile car phone. She wanted him to stop at the cleaners.

"Hi, Herb. Mrs. Jetson said I should pick up my suit."

"Sure thing. Here it is."

"Thanks, Herb. Put it on my bill."

"Gee, that suit looks a lot like the one Harlan brought in," Herb said to himself as George was leaving.

When George arrived at the Jetsons' sky pad, Elroy was busy splitting atoms again!

"Hi, Dad. Want to be the first to try my new anti-gravity wrist watch?"

"Not now, Elroy. I gotta change my suit." George thought the clean suit had shrunk a little.

"Please, Dad, try it. Then you can fly around the room."

"Okay, okay." George agreed to go along with the joke.
"Anti-gravity watches—what a—Hey! I'm flying! Yow-ee!
Elroy, you're a genius!"
Jane and Judy couldn't believe their eyes!
"I gotta show Spacely," said George. "He'll make me a
vice-president. We'll be rich!"

Mr. Spacely was shocked to see George flying by his window! "Jetson! What's going on?" Spacely barked.

"My son Elroy invented this anti-gravity watch, sir. Just put it on your wrist and you can fly!"

"Really?"

"Absolutely! Want to join me in a flight around the building?" asked George.

"You know, Jetson, old pal, I've always thought you ought to be a vice-president. Maybe even get a raise. I'd like to see Cogswell top this!"

At Cosmic Cogs it was time to demonstrate the X-1500 suit for the Board. Cogswell promised them a smooth, fast, quiet flight.

"But, Mr. Cogswell, it doesn't work!" Harlan said.

"Don't give me that! Now make like a bird, will you!"

"HELP!"

"I can't believe it!" said Cogswell. "The flying suit has bombed!"

.267

Harlan took the suit back to the cleaners, but there was no hurry this time.

"Hey, this is Mr. Jetson's suit," said Herb. "I'd better get over there with it right away."

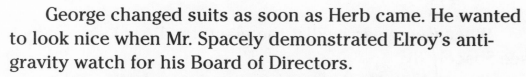

George changed suits as soon as Herb came. He wanted to look nice when Mr. Spacely demonstrated Elroy's anti-gravity watch for his Board of Directors.

George buckled on the watch, opened the window, and started to fly off.

"HELP! HELP!"

"George, what happened?" Jane asked.

"This anti-gravity watch isn't working! Boy, this was the shortest vice-presidency in history!"

269

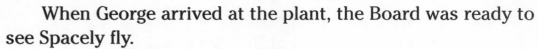

When George arrived at the plant, the Board was ready to see Spacely fly.

"Don't do it, Mr. Spacely," George begged. "Don't do it!"

"Be quiet, Jetson! Now watch me, ladies and gentlemen. I put on the watch and . . . Geronimo!"

"Well, Jetson, without that watch, it means the end of Spacely Sprockets. Cogswell can buy this company!" Mr. Spacely was ready to give up.

But Mr. Cogswell didn't need Spacely Sprockets any longer. When Harlan brought the X-1500 suit back from the cleaners, Cogswell told him to throw it out the window.

It was soon picked up by the window washer.

"Hey, nothing like a new suit to give a guy a lift!" the man said.

On his way home, George made a big decision.

"No more get-rich-quick schemes for me! If I never see people fly, it'll be too soon for me!"

A Date with Jet Screamer

It's almost dinner time at the Jetsons, and George has zoomed in from another hard day of pushing buttons at the Spacely Sprocket Company.

Jane greeted him as he came through the space port.

"Hello, honey. Bad day at the office?"

"Yeah, these three-hour days are killing me," George said. "Hey, what's going on here?"

"Judy's friends are having a meeting of the Jet Screamer fan club. He's on TV."

"Not Jet Screamer again!" George exploded. "I will not put up with that noise!"

"But, George, Judy has to listen to you when you play your drums," Jane said.

"That's different. I play *music* on the drums. Now I want quiet!"

After the house was clear and quiet again, George went to have a little talk with Judy. She was busy doing homework, or so George thought.

"Oh, Dad, I'm writing these great song lyrics for the Jet Screamer song contest. If my song wins, I get to go out with him on a real date. I can't lose!"

"Listen, young lady, we're stopping everything on Jet Screamer. No more tapes, no more pictures, no more Jet Screamer—period! Now get back to your homework!" George's words were final.

Elroy was coming out of the shower and spin-dry cycle when George asked him what he and his friends had been playing that day.

"We were writing messages in secret code, Dad. See?"

George read, "Eep, Opp, Ork, Ah, Ah—in secret code, eh? That means 'Meet me tonight'."

"Dad, that's a secret!"

"Well, it's no secret that your mother will bop us if we're late for supper. Come on."

277

Just before bedtime, Judy asked her mother to mail an envelope for her the next morning. It was addressed to the Jet Screamer Song Writing Contest. George decided to take care of the contest right then. He took out Judy's entry and replaced it with Elroy's secret code message.

"We've got a guaranteed loser!" he told Jane.

One day a few weeks later Judy rushed home to turn on the TV. George tried to tell her that her chances of winning the contest were very slim. Then Jet Screamer appeared on the screen.

"I'd like to sing the winning song written by Miss Judy Jetson. The song is called "EEP, OPP, ORK, AH AH," which means 'we've got a date tomorrow night, Judy!'"

"Mom, Mom! I won! I won!" Judy cried. "I've got a date with Jet Screamer!"

"Hey, Dad, he knows my secret code," said Elroy.

George couldn't answer either of them. He had fainted in the chair.

EEP-OPP-ORK AH-AH MEANS "MEET ME TONIGHT"

BLOOP-BABBA BOOP-BLIP MEANS "DON'T BE LATE"

When Jet Screamer arrived the next day, he was not alone. Television cameras filled the Jetsons' living room. The announcer introduced Jet Screamer himself and Jet's date for the night—Judy Jetson. Then he turned to George.

"And how does it feel to be the father of the winner?"

"I feel . . . I feel . . . I feel . . ." George was speechless.

FUN PAD

But after Judy and Jet left, George started to worry again. "My daughter's going to have a chaperone—whether she likes it or not!" he said to Jane.

Jet and Judy headed for the Fun Pad where Jet sang in the Swivel Lounge every night. George was not far behind them.

At the back of the club, George found the drummer at the stage entrance.

Inside Jet Screamer introduced his band members one by one. "And on the drums . . ."

"It's Daddy!" cried Judy. "What's he doing here?"

"He's a fan, baby. And if he can play the drums, I'll make him a star tonight!"

Jet turned to the audience. "Tune in, Swivelers! Have I got a treat for you. A new song by Judy Jetson! And on the boom booms—Space Dust Daddy himself!"

"Who—me?" asked George.

"You can do it, Daddy! Go get 'em!" Judy called.

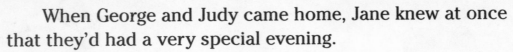

When George and Judy came home, Jane knew at once that they'd had a very special evening.

"What's going on, George?" she asked.

"Darling, darling, darling, ah, ah, ah," answered George.

"Look, Mom," cried Judy. "Here's the new president of the Jet Screamer Fan Club!"

"EEP, OPP, ORK, AH AH," sang George, "that means I love you."